A PERILOUS WAGER

The Willowbrook Series
Book 5

By Laura Landon

ARE YOU SIGNED UP FOR DRAGONBLADE'S BLOG?

You'll get the latest news and information on exclusive giveaways, exclusive excerpts, coming releases, sales, free books, cover reveals and more.

Check out our complete list of authors, too!

No spam, no junk. That's a promise!

Sign Up Here

www.dragonbladepublishing.com

Dearest Reader;

Thank you for your support of a small press. At Dragonblade Publishing, we strive to bring you the highest quality Historical Romance from some of the best authors in the business. Without your support, there is no 'us', so we sincerely hope you adore these stories and find some new favorite authors along the way.

Happy Reading!

CEO, Dragonblade Publishing

Additional Dragonblade books by Author Laura Landon

The Willowbrook Series
A Willowbrook Miracle (Book 1)
A Page Turner Bookshop (Book 2)
A Bitter Pill to Swallow (Book 3)
A Lesson Learned (Book 4)
A Perilous Wager (Book 5)

Men of Valor Series
A Love For All Time (Book 1)
A Love That Knows No Bounds (Book 2)
A Love That's Worth The Risk (Book 3)
A Love That Heals the Heart (Book 4)

PROLOGUE

Crimean War
April 1855

MAJOR JACKSON CORBIN huddled in the corner of the Russian prison and clasped his hands over his ears. He did everything he could to block out the screams of pain coming from his fellow officer and best friend, Lieutenant Bradford Prescott. Brad was paying the price for what Jack had done. Or rather, for what Jack knew.

Another bloodcurdling scream echoed off the stone walls. Jack bit back a cry of anguish that threatened to cast up the contents of his stomach. Except there wasn't anything to cast up. It had been days since they'd been fed, and the little food they were given wasn't edible.

Jack pressed his hands over his ears again to dull the cries of torture. He couldn't stand to listen to the pain the Russians were inflicting on his friend to force Brad to reveal secrets the young soldier didn't know.

Jack was the only one who knew where the army would attack next. Except, if he didn't return to headquarters, no one would know.

Hopefully, when Jack didn't return, his commanding officer would realize he'd most likely been captured and would come to rescue him. But he was afraid that by that time there would be no one left to rescue.

Jack sucked in a deep breath when another anguished scream echoed in the cold, damp dungeon.

"Does it bother you to hear your friend suffer, Major? Or does it not affect you to know that you are the cause of the lieutenant's agony?"

Jack lifted his head and glared at the Russian officer who had ordered Brad's torture.

"You bloody bastard," Jack answered with all his bitterness flooding his voice. "You know bloody well Lieutenant Prescott doesn't know anything. I'm the only one who has the information you want."

"Of course you are," the Russian officer said with a grin of satisfaction on his face. "But we've already tried to *encourage* you to share your secrets with us, and you refused. It would hardly be to our benefit if we killed you in the process of getting the information we want. You have a tolerance for pain that far surpasses that of any British soldier I've ever seen. Now we will see if you are equally as able to listen to your young officer suffer the pain that should have been yours."

Before Jack could respond, several guards dragged Brad back into the cell and dropped him at Jack's feet.

"We stopped, for now," one of the guards said as he locked the cell door behind him. "It seemed useless to torture an unconscious man."

The guards laughed as they left the dungeon.

"I'll let you tend to your friend," the commanding officer said, then left with a vile grin and a swagger in his step.

Jack was filled with a hatred that only intensified when he looked at Brad. "I'll make them pay," he whispered.

Jack ripped off a piece of his shredded uniform and dipped it in the little water left from earlier in the day. He dabbed at the blood streaming down Brad's broken jaw in an effort to ease his pain. They'd whipped him with a cat-o'-nine-tails. Its nine knotted cords had cruelly peeled several strips of skin from his back, shoulders, and face.

Jack had a strong constitution, but seeing his friend's skin torn from his body was more than he could stomach. "This is the last time they'll touch you, friend," he swore as he gently patted at the blood oozing from raw flesh.

Brad moaned in pain, and Jack held a cup of water to his lips.

"I can…handle…another round…"

"Maybe you can, friend, but I can't," Jack said.

"What are you…going to…do?"

"Whatever it takes, Lieutenant. You just lie still and watch the show."

"Help…should come…soon," Brad said in pain-filled gasps.

Jack poured the last of the water over Brad's back. "Not soon enough," he said. "Not soon enough." He did as much as he could to stop the worst of the bleeding, then sat down on the filthy floor, leaned against the wall…and waited.

He tried to regain as much strength as he could before the enemy returned. He'd need all he could muster to inflict as much damage as possible. He wouldn't survive, he knew he wouldn't, but neither would as many of their vile enemy as he could eliminate.

He closed his eyes and summoned a vision of what he had hoped would be his future. He knew now that it would never happen, his dream to open his own gentlemen's club. It would be a prestigious establishment catering to an upper tier of men in a community that didn't have any other place for them to gather socially. His club would serve the finest food and alcohol, and there would be a room for members to sit and relax and read newspapers, engage in conversation and lively debate. There would be another lavishly appointed room reserved for gambling and card games. Perhaps there would even be a few rooms on the upper floor with female entertainment.

Everything in his establishment would be of the finest quality, and members would have to meet certain requirements to belong.

A smile lifted the corners of Jack's mouth as he fleshed out his dream, but it quickly faded when he heard the clomp of heavy boots on the stone steps that led below ground to his gloomy cell. They were coming back. But this call would be their last.

"Pretend you're unconscious, Brad. Don't move."

"What are you…going to…do?"

"Let me handle this," he said, wrapping the chains they'd used to confine him around his hands. They were the only weapon he had to use against them.

"No, Jack," Brad struggled to say. "You don't stand…a chance."

"Neither do you if I don't do something."

"No…" Brad said again.

"Quiet," Jack whispered.

The footsteps from beyond their cell grew louder, and Jack said a quick prayer that this would be over quickly, then waited for the cell door to open.

Three guards entered, and Jack tightened his grip on the chain binding his hands. They approached Brad, and one of the guards bent down to grab him.

"I don't know why we're wasting our time with this one. He doesn't know anything, and he's close to death already. We should concentrate on the other one and leave this one to die on his own."

A second guard grunted his agreement, and a third made what must have been a lewd remark, judging from the way the three Russians laughed. They turned their attention away from Brad.

Jack was ready. When they were near enough, he let out a crazed bellow, pulled his arm back as far as the chain would allow, and released the chain as he swung his arm forward.

The chain wasn't long, but it was long enough that it slashed through the air and struck two of the guards across their faces, knocking them to the ground. In the next instant, he kicked out and caught the third fellow on the jaw with the side of his boot.

The guards released painful bellows that echoed in the dungeon, loud enough that Jack was sure they could be heard throughout the prison.

He yanked at the chain, ready to send it flying again, but it was caught on the foot of one of the downed guards. Before he could recover it, the Russian commander charged into the cell. The guards recovered enough to unite against him.

The three guards surrounded him, and while Jack fought off one of his attackers, the second and third pulled out knives and guns to use against him.

The enemy to his right lifted his gun and took aim. Jack staggered, and just as he whirled away, a bullet entered his back. Before he could recover his balance, he felt the piercing pain of a knife as it sliced through the flesh at his side. He pushed away from the wall, fought the first guard and knocked him to the ground, then went after the second.

Blood streamed from his back and side, and even though he weakened with each wound he suffered, he managed to stay on his feet and fight off his attackers. In his rage he felt flooded with a power he'd never known before.

"Behind you, Jack!"

He heard Brad warn him just as the third guard sliced his flesh open below his right shoulder. A searing pain ripped through him, clear to his waist.

He knew this wound would probably cause his death. But before he could give in to it, he watched in resigned terror as the commanding officer aimed his pistol and fired a bullet that struck him in the shoulder. Jack felt himself fall to the ground just as Brad's voice penetrated the melee.

"Help's coming!" his friend cried, but Jack was afraid the arrival of a rescue party was too late to save him.

Jack welcomed the cold stone floor and gave in to the darkness that consumed him. At least Brad would be spared another round of torture.

CHAPTER ONE

1863
Village of Willowbrook

MAGDALENA OSBOURNE CLUTCHED her meager bundles to her chest and rushed home with a smile lighting her face. Her baskets and bundles that had held buns and loaves of bread earlier that morning were now empty. This had turned out to be a very good day. She could almost forget how tired she was. Almost.

"Is that you, Miss Lena?" Mattie, hired to watch over Lena's sister Esther, smiled as she came out into the kitchen to discover why Lena was home so soon.

Lena had left the house at daybreak to deliver the dinner rolls she'd spent nearly the whole night baking. Usually Annie, who owned Annie's Restaurant, took some of them, and Lena would set up a stand on the corner across from the Page Turner Bookshop to sell the rest. But this morning, Annie had taken all Lena's dinner rolls, with a promise that she'd take another batch if Lena could get them delivered by midafternoon.

It seemed that a delegation from London, along with several local investors, was to meet to discuss the creation of a railroad line extending from London to Willowbrook and beyond. Annie was anticipating an increase in business as long as the delegation was in Willowbrook.

"I have exciting news," Lena said, getting out her bowls to begin a second batch of bread. "Where is Esther?"

"I'm here," Esther answered, coming around the corner. She wasn't dressed for the day, and still wore her robe and slippers. "I wasn't expecting you back already. What exciting news do you have?"

Lena began setting out the ingredients for another batch of dough and shared her news about the possibility of a railroad going through Willowbrook.

"I can't believe such talk might finally become a reality," Esther said with more excitement than Lena had seen from her sister since their mother passed away nearly a year ago. "Do you know what that means, Lena? We'll be able to go to London for supplies we can't get here in Willowbrook."

"And what supplies would those be?" Lena teased. "There's nothing we need that we can't get in Willowbrook."

"There might be," Esther answered. "We don't even know what there is in London. We've never been there."

"And there's every chance that we will never get there. We'll both be very old ladies by the time a railroad gets built."

"I guess you're right," Esther said with a sigh.

Lena regretted her lack of excitement. Esther had so little to look forward to in life, and this was one more dream Lena had thoughtlessly wrenched from her grasp.

"Although it might get built much faster than I think. There are several locals with an interest in having a connection with London."

"Yes," Esther said with a smile. "Anyone with a wife and daughters who want the latest fashions in gowns."

"No, silly. I was thinking about every farmer in the area with grain or livestock to get to market."

"You're always so practical, Lena."

"Well, one of us has to be," Lena countered, then realized how sharp her comment sounded.

"I'm sorry, Esther. I didn't mean to snap at you. I'm just tired." Lena finished mixing her dough and placed a cloth over the bowl, then set it closer to the oven, where the warmth would help it rise. "I'm going to lie down for a bit. Would you call me when the dough has doubled in size so I can push it down?"

"Why don't you let Esther and me take care of that?" Mattie said. "We'll call you when the dough is ready to form into buns."

"You are dears!" Lena cried as she hurried to her room. She couldn't wait to get into bed and close her eyes. She felt as though it had been forever since she'd slept, and according to Annie, the delegation from London would be in Willowbrook for close to a month. That meant she would be on this schedule for several weeks. She couldn't complain about the extra money she would make, but she couldn't expect Mattie to spend all that time with Esther. She had responsibilities of her own to take care of at home, and Esther needed someone with her all the time. That left Lena to do the baking and delivering.

JACK CORBIN CAST his eye around the room he'd configured for business meetings at his gentlemen's club. He had designed the room similar to several elegantly appointed meeting rooms he'd encountered in London and Edinburgh. This was just the fourth gathering of the prestigious railroad group, and he was satisfied he'd met his mark in preparing for them.

He took his place at the long central table along with six other influential men from Willowbrook and an entourage of investors from London, mostly railroad owners and industry moguls. As the owner of Jackson's Gentlemen's Club, one of the most profitable establishments in Willowbrook, he would play a major role in such a massive improvement to the town, and had offered his rooms for their meetings. He was satisfied with his efforts, seeing the appreciative looks on the faces of men who he knew were some of London's elite. Several had even found the new cigar cabinets he'd placed discreetly about the room, and had already made it their habit to appreciatively sample the excellent brands Jack stocked them with.

Since he'd started the club nearly two years earlier, it had grown from a struggling establishment, with just two or three customers a day, to having every room packed with patrons. Many came daily to enjoy the peace and quiet of a relaxing atmosphere where they could read their newspapers and broadsheets away from the bustle of family life. They could visit the card rooms for a bit of gambling, or eat in the dining areas, where they could get an excellent meal and drink the finest liquor.

Jackson's Gentlemen's Club had turned into one of the most popular places in Willowbrook, as well as one of the most profitable. Jack was raking in more money than he'd ever imagined, and Brad had been at his side from day one. Therefore, it was not surprising that he had been included in the meetings with investors wanting to establish a railroad to connect Willowbrook with London.

The two groups had been in heavy discussions for the past week and a half. The railroad investors had already done much of the preliminary work needed. They'd hired surveyors to assess the best route for the railroad to take to reach Willowbrook, and what land they would have to acquire to lay the tracks. They had already lined up most of the finances needed to hire the necessary workers and purchase materials.

Jack was impressed with what had been done and listened with rapt attention, since a large portion of the land they intended to buy ran through an estate he'd purchased less than a year ago. Although he wasn't sure his purchase of the estate was common knowledge in Willowbrook, it would net him a tidy profit if the railroad decided to buy it.

The president of the railroad investors from London was a Mr. Wilson Hanover. He was very organized and knew every detail of the facts he presented with unerring accuracy—but for some reason Jack couldn't explain, he didn't like the man. Perhaps it was because of his refusal to listen to anyone else's point of view. Or perhaps it was just a personality difference between them. But it hardly mattered.

The second investor who was quite vocal with his opinion was a man called Josiah Barnaby. It was obvious from the first day that the two men were at loggerheads over several details, including the railroad's route, as well as the estimated date of completion.

Jack sat back in his chair, listened to everything, and evaluated the feasibility of their ideas. Every once in a while, one of the members asked for an opinion, but Jack let the other members speak for the group rather than offering one himself.

"Don't you have anything to offer, Major Corbin?"

Jack cast a glance around the table and met everyone's gaze with a seriousness that demanded their attention. Many still addressed him as major, and a corner of his mind appreciated that sign of respect.

"One lesson I learned early on in the military, gentlemen, was that it was vital to gather all the facts before offering an opinion on anything. During the war, making a decision before knowing all the facts could cost hundreds of innocent soldiers their lives."

A silence descended over the gathering, stealing the argumentative direction their conversation had been headed.

"Sage advice, Major Corbin," the Earl of Murdock, the Duke of Willowbrook's heir, said. "So, is there any information you would like before we continue? If we can share it, we will. If not, we should appoint someone to gather it before our next meeting."

Jack dropped his spent cigar into a crystal ashtray he'd imported from Bavaria. "Actually, there is. Several of the delegation from London have indicated that there are decisions that will be made at a later time by those elected to the governing board of the railroad. Exactly who will be on this governing board? Equal representation by the London investors and an elected citizenry from Willowbrook?"

"Well…" Hanover said, clearly at a loss for words.

Jack cast a glance in Barnaby's direction. "Do you know the answer to that question, Mr. Barnaby?"

"Well, yes. I think it was decided that the governing board would be made up of seven members, six from the London investors, since they are the ones who will contribute the greatest share of the financing, and one from the citizens of Willowbrook."

"I hesitate to speak for the citizens of Willowbrook, but I can't imagine they would agree to that ratio on the board."

There was a murmur of agreement from the residents of Willowbrook.

"I think we should have equal representation," the Earl of Murdock said. "If you suggest seven members, then I propose that four of them be representatives of Willowbrook, and three of them from the London investors."

"Are you suggesting that there be more board members from Willowbrook than from the London investors, Lord Murdock?" Barnaby asked.

"I am. Since the citizens of Willowbrook will have to assume most of the care and maintenance of the rails, as well as make sure the surrounding pastureland is fenced off from the tracks, provide relay housing for engineers and coal tenders, provide workers to offload freight, and clear and repair tracks and so on, I think that is only fair."

There was a decisive murmur from the group, both pro and con.

"You haven't even asked your members if there are enough of them who can raise the amount necessary to finance such a venture," Barnaby said with a smug expression.

"What amount are we talking about?" the Lord Murdock asked.

Hanover sat forward in his chair and stated an amount that

was astronomical, but not beyond reach for many of them.

"May I see a show of hands?" Jack said. "How many can commit to such an amount?"

Spencer Washburn, Earl of Carnhaven, raised a regal finger.

Hunter Melbourne, Earl of Murdock, lifted a hand and nodded. "I will also commit that amount from my grandfather, the Duke of Willowbrook."

Jack raised his hand as well.

"And I also suggest the village of Willowbrook will commit to a share," Lord Murdock said. "I assume a profit will be made from the railroad. The village can always use extra income for community improvements."

"As you can see," Jack said, "the people of Willowbrook could finance the railroad without your help, Mr. Hanover. We do, however, require your knowledge and your expertise. Therefore, we encourage your participation."

"Our members will take your suggestion under advisement," Hanover replied.

There was an uncomfortable pause that took several moments to recover from. Finally, Hanover asked the next question. "Are there any other details upon which you need clarification?"

"Actually, there are," Jack said.

Hanover actually smiled. "Somehow I thought there would be."

The occupants of the room chuckled, though only on the Willowbrook side.

"Who will be responsible for keeping the accounts and sending out the billings? I assume since nearly all the business will be transacted from here, it would be prudent to have the business office located here as well."

"Are you volunteering for the position, Major Corbin?" Barnaby asked.

"If there is not a better candidate, then yes, I can handle the job. I will expect someone of your choosing to audit the transactions and go over the books at least once a quarter."

"Yes, I'm sure we would all demand that."

"Of course."

They voted, and Jack was elected the representative to keep the accounts and pay the bills.

"Are there any other points of discussion?" Hanover asked.

"Perhaps we've made enough decisions for today," the Lord Murdock said when no one seemed eager to bring up another concern.

"That sounds like an excellent suggestion," Hanover said. "Until tomorrow, then."

The London investors rose and filed out of the room. Jack followed them to close the door so the Willowbrook delegation would have privacy to talk when they were alone. Because he was standing at the door, Jack overheard a comment between Hanover and Barnaby.

"I thought you said the men from Willowbrook were so desperate to have a railroad that they'd go along with anything we told them?"

"Seems I underestimated them," Hanover answered. "We'll have to be careful to maintain the upper hand."

CHAPTER TWO

THE FOLLOWING WEEK flew by so fast that Lena lost track of the days. She worked through the night to bake the first batch of bread and buns, then carried them the near mile into Willowbrook to deliver them to Annie's Restaurant. Then she rushed back home and started her second batch of bread.

Some evenings she caught a few hours of sleep, but more often she didn't.

Esther tried to keep her company most of the time when she was baking, but it was hard for her. She didn't have anything to do, and Lena would look to where Esther sat and find her sleeping.

Lena would smile at the sight of her sister struggling to stay awake. Her eyes would close, her head would drop to her crossed arms on the table, and it wasn't long before she would fall into a deep sleep.

There was something angelic about her when she slept. Lena wondered if everyone looked so peaceful when they slept, or if it was only Esther.

She finished mixing her dough then placed it near the oven to let it rise. On her way back to the table, she stopped to brush a wisp of hair that had fallen across Esther's brow.

Her sister was only a year and a half younger than Lena's six and twenty, and she looked much like their mother, with blonde hair and blue eyes, while Lena took after their father, with dark hair and eyes so dark they were nearly black. They were both quite attractive, although Esther was by far the prettier of the two.

She was the picture of perfection, except for her one flaw—a flaw Lena couldn't fix or make go away.

Esther was born blind, so she didn't know the beauty of the earth. She'd never seen the sun, but she'd felt its warmth. She'd never seen the rain, but she recognized its wetness. She'd never seen the printed word, but she loved to listen to Lena read to her, probably more than she enjoyed anything else.

When they were young, Esther would hold out her hand and wait for Lena to reach for it. Lena was her eyes, and she tried to show her sister every inch of the world around her. As she grew older, Esther had gained an independence that Lena marveled at. She could walk around their small cottage without running into anything. It was as if she sensed where obstacles were and knew where to step to avoid them.

Unfortunately, there were many everyday tasks she couldn't do. Or perhaps she could if Lena allowed her to attempt them, such as cooking, but Lena wouldn't let her take the risks that went along with it, such as getting burned, or starting a fire and not being able to put it out.

No, Lena protected her sister as much as she could, just as their mother had when she was alive, and her father had when he was here with them. But he'd been gone these past ten years, which was why paying their bills was so difficult. At least they had a house to live in for a while yet.

Their father had been the vicar in Willowbrook for more than fifteen years, long before it began to grow. The congregation had allowed his widow and daughters to stay in the house after he was no longer there to serve as their vicar. Lena wasn't sure what the congregation intended to do now that their mother was gone, too.

Willowbrook was growing so rapidly that it was only a matter of time until another vicar was needed. She was certain that then she and Essie would be asked to find a different place to live so they could use this cottage to house a new vicar.

Lena wasn't sure what they would do then. It wasn't as if they could live lives like other women. It wasn't as if they could have the dreams that other females had. Husbands and families were not part of their future. It was obvious that Esther would never marry, and Lena's chances of finding someone who would take on a wife with a blind sister were almost nonexistent.

Lena sat at the table opposite Esther and closed her eyes as the dough rose. Her life was so simple, yet complicated at the moment. This added job of providing bread and buns for the restaurant was such a blessing, but according to Annie, it would soon come to an end. The London investors were due to return home next week, and construction was supposed to begin the following week. According to Annie, that was when her restaurant would return to normal, and Lena would not have to bake nearly as much bread.

The only man who would be busier than now was Jackson Corbin. He'd been given the responsibility of keeping the books and overseeing the finances of the construction of the railroad. He was the owner of Willowbrook's popular gentlemen's club, and Lena couldn't imagine the added responsibility of keeping the railroad accounts. She was just glad that *she* didn't have that responsibility.

"ARE YOU STILL working on the railroad ledgers, Jack?"

Jack looked up to see his friend and partner Brad Prescott standing in the doorway. "Come in. Distract me for a minute. Tell me what is going on in the club I own but haven't seen the inside of since this railroad consumed my attention."

Brad chuckled, then entered the room and closed the door

behind him. "We've been quite busy lately," he said when he sat in his usual chair across from Jack. "Everyone wants to hear the latest news about the railroad, and where better to hear that news than here?"

"Ah, yes," Jack said, rubbing the back of his neck. "So, how are *you* doing, Brad?"

"That's why I'm here, Jack. I need help. You know numbers are not my strength. I'm doing the best I can, but I'm having trouble keeping up. I know you can't do more than you're already doing, so I thought perhaps we might consider finding someone else to fill in, at least with the club's books. I know you want to concentrate on the railroad books, at least until the railroad gets up and running, and I will keep an eye on the club's books so they get done right, but I can't do more right now."

"I know, Brad. You didn't sign on for this added responsibility."

"I signed on for whatever you need me to do. I'm alive because of you. If not for what you did in that Russian prison, I'd be one of the casualties of war."

"Your bravery is what made you one of the survivors."

Brad gave him the same look he always did when Jack paid him a compliment. Because of the horrific wounds he'd suffered in that Russian prison, he was immensely self-conscious. The wide scar that ran from his temple down the right side of his face to below his jaw had changed his looks, and he still hadn't regained his confidence.

He seldom left the club. He didn't feel comfortable going out in public, and Jack didn't blame him.

People were cruel. They avoided looking at him, and they often shielded their eyes to avoid having to make eye contact.

The club was the only place where he felt comfortable. The men who frequented Jackson's Gentlemen's Club knew him and were used to him.

"So, getting back to your concern. What are you suggesting we do?"

Brad sat forward in his chair. "I'd like you to consider hiring another person to do the accounts for the club."

Jack pondered the request. He'd always been of the opinion that he and Brad should handle the finances by themselves. Jack wanted to keep the amount of money the club made between the two of them. He didn't want word to get out concerning the amount that Jackson's Gentlemen's Club took in, or the amounts its members made or lost at its betting tables.

"I know you never wanted anyone else to see our books or know our income, or how much our clients owe, but things are different now, Jack. That was when we thought that you would always be here to shoulder half of the responsibility."

Brad's last words struck a nerve. He was correct. Jack wasn't shouldering his half. "Do you have anyone in mind to work with us?"

"I have a few suggestions, but that decision will be up to you."

"Who are you suggesting?"

"I thought we might consider Rupert Longsworth. He keeps the books for Jasper and Son, one of the largest retailers in Willowbrook."

Jack thought a moment, then shook his head. "Not him," he answered. "Not only is he a client here, but he has a penchant for gambling and owes us quite a sum. Anyone else?"

"It's a female. Miss Magdalena Osbourne."

"A woman?"

"Yes. Her father was the vicar here for several years."

"Who recommended her?"

"Annie, from the restaurant. Annie says she's a hard worker and as honest as the day is long. She's also very intelligent."

"I've never heard of her," Jack said.

"You wouldn't have. She seldom leaves her home. She took care of her ailing mother until she passed last year, and now cares for her sister."

"What's wrong with her sister?"

"I don't know. She must be an invalid, too."

Jack thought for a moment.

"Will you at least speak to her, Jack? You don't have to hire her. Just talk to her."

"Very well," Jack finally said. "Let me know where she lives, and I'll go see her tomorrow."

"Thank you," Brad said, and left the office.

Jack tried to get back to work but couldn't concentrate on the figures in front of him. All he could think about was hiring a female to work in a gentlemen's club. It was something he'd sworn he would never do, other than in a position to entertain the male guests. But he owed it to Brad to at least go see the lady. He had no intention of offering her a position, but at least he could tell his friend he'd talked to her.

He initially intended to talk to her tomorrow, but decided to get this distasteful task over today. He already knew what her answer would be. She was a vicar's daughter, after all, and wouldn't consider working in a gentlemen's club. He'd call on her, thank her for considering his offer, then leave her, never to see her again.

Jack found out where she lived, then walked the mile to the Osbourne cottage. He paused to consider exactly what he intended to say to the lady. He would offer her the position of secretary in charge of keeping Jackson's Gentlemen's Club's ledgers. He expected her to refuse his offer outright, and vowed to accept her refusal without argument.

The more he thought about hiring a female for such a position, the more he realized what a bad idea this was. His business was for gentlemen only. The rooms on the first floor were legitimate, if you considered gambling a legitimate pastime, but those on the second floor were anything but. And Miss Osbourne was no doubt a strait-laced vicar's daughter. He couldn't imagine her accepting his proposition.

He took a deep breath, lifted his hand, and knocked on the door.

No one answered, so he knocked again, this time a little louder.

He listened, and finally heard footsteps approaching from inside.

Slowly, the knob turned and the door opened, and Jack found himself looking at the most alluring features imaginable. The woman standing in front of him was remarkably beautiful.

Her hair was the most luxurious shade of deep, rich brown, and her large, round eyes were so dark they almost looked black. But what caught his attention most were the big, wet tears that threatened to spill down her cheeks. For some reason, Miss Osbourne had been crying. And even more disturbing was the fact that Jack had to clench his hands at his sides to keep from reaching out to her, wrapping her in his arms, and holding her.

CHAPTER THREE

"Oh, I'm sorry," she said. "I shouldn't have answered the door. I just thought you might be…"

"I might be who?" Jack asked when she didn't finish her sentence.

"The men who were just here."

"There were men here?" he asked. "Did they bother you? Are you all right?"

"Oh, yes. I just…" She paused when a fresh batch of tears spilled down her cheeks. "I'm sorry," she said. "I just received some distressing news, and I haven't had time to adjust to it yet. I'll be fine in a moment."

Jack watched her try to put on a brave face and fail.

"May I help you?" she asked.

"I'm Major Jackson Corbin," he said. "I own Jackson's Gentlemen's Club, and I'd like to speak with you, Miss Osbourne. May I come in?"

"I…I don't know. I…"

"I will only take a moment of your time."

"Very well," she said when she recovered from the surprise of hearing his name. She stepped back from the door and allowed him to enter. "Please, come in."

She led him to a small room that appeared to serve as the home's receiving room. "Please, have a seat. Would you like some tea?"

"No, thank you. I won't be here that long. I just came to ask you a question."

She turned to face him. "Yes, Mr. Corbin?"

"As I said, I am the owner of Jackson's Gentlemen's Club. I was also recently appointed chief financial officer for the railroad project that will connect Willowbrook with London. The task I was assigned is quite time consuming, and I find that doing the books for both the railroad and the club is quite overwhelming. I would therefore like to offer you a position working in the gentlemen's club."

"A position?" she said, her eyebrows lifting and her forehead furrowing.

He could tell she had no idea what position he was talking about and assumed it might be one of the women that entertained men in the upstairs rooms.

"Please," he said, interrupting her before she asked him to leave. "Let me explain. I am in need of a secretary. Someone to help me with the accounts. All you would be hired to do is keep a record of the daily intake of the club, and make up a deposit to take to the bank every day."

She turned away from him and sat in the nearest chair. Jack moved to sit in the one opposite her.

"I apologize for giving you the wrong impression, but let me assure you, you would not have anything to do with what transpires in the club. You would have your own office where you would do your work and not interact with any of the customers. In fact, you won't even be allowed to enter the club. We have a very strict rule against allowing any females inside the establishment."

"Let me stop you right there, Mr. Corbin. I'm afraid I have to refuse your offer of employment."

A voice in the back of his head told him to accept her refusal. That had been his intent from the first moment he left the club to talk to her. But when he opened his mouth, acceptance of her refusal wasn't what tumbled out.

"But you haven't even heard the terms of my proposal. I assure you, they are very generous."

"I'm sure they are, sir. But in all honesty, I could not accept any offer you made."

"May I ask why, Miss Osbourne?"

Jack was forced to watch her eyes mist over. He decided at that moment that he wouldn't accept her refusal. He intended to help her. No matter what trouble she was in, he would come to her aid.

"The men who were here before you arrived were representatives of the church. They came to inform me that a new vicar has been hired and will arrive in two weeks. We have to be out of the cottage before then."

"They are kicking you out of your home?" Jack couldn't believe it. "Do you have someplace else to go?"

She shook her head. "Not yet. I will have to search for a home."

"What will you use for income?"

She stared at her clenched hands in her lap and shook her head.

"Please, let me help you," Jack said, placing his hand over her locked fingers.

"You don't even know me," she said, lifting her damp eyes to look at him.

His heart melted. "That doesn't matter, Miss Osbourne. You are in trouble, and so am I. I need your assistance."

"Why me?" she asked.

Jack thought for several moments before he answered. "Because you have no connection to me or my establishment. My club allows only men, and since you are not a man," he said with a smile on his face, "you cannot run up a huge gambling debt and be forced to steal to repay it."

"Steal?" she asked.

"Yes," he replied. "Forced to steal from the club to repay your debt."

"Oh." Miss Osbourne's mouth formed a perfect circle.

Jack couldn't tear his gaze away from her lips.

"I can offer you my guarantee that I will never steal from you. I will never take anything that isn't mine, sir. That was one thing my father was very firm on. That is one of God's commandments. Thou shalt not steal."

Jack couldn't help but smile. "Your father followed the commandments."

"My father was the vicar here. He followed all God's commandments."

"Then I see that I will not have to be concerned with you stealing," Jack said in a teasing tone. "So, does that mean you will accept my offer?"

He knew from the torn expression on her face that she still intended to refuse him. That was what he wanted, wasn't it? So why did he have this overwhelming desire to stop the words before she spoke them?

"Do you have another source of income you can rely on?" he asked.

She shook her head.

"Then why are you hesitating?"

"It's not only me I'm concerned with, Mr. Corbin."

"Who else are you responsible for?"

"My sister, Esther."

"How old is your sister?"

"I am older by a year."

"And she is not married?"

Miss Osbourne shook her head again.

"Would you introduce us?"

"You want to meet her?"

"It would be my pleasure."

"Very well. Follow me."

Miss Osbourne led him from the room, through a small hallway, and into another small room that looked as if it served as a library. On the outer wall there was a multi-paned door that she opened. That door led to a well-kept garden with a variety of flowers in bloom.

"Esther," she called out when they neared a young lady who sat on a wrought-iron bench at the side of the path.

The lady turned with a smile, and Jack got his first look at a female who was the nearest image of an angel he'd ever seen.

Miss Osbourne walked close to her sister and took her hand. "Esther, we have a guest."

"Oh," Esther said, and even though she did not look at Jack, the smile on her face became broader.

"Yes, I'd like to introduce you to Mr. Jackson Corbin. Mr. Corbin, meet my sister, Miss Esther Osbourne."

"How do you do, Mr. Corbin?" she said in the sweetest voice Jack had ever heard.

"It's a pleasure to meet you," Jack said. Esther didn't look at him until he spoke, but then she focused her full attention on him.

"Are you from Willowbrook?" she asked with genuine inter-est.

"Yes. I own Jackson's Gentlemen's Club."

"Oh, how exciting. That is where men can go to gamble, isn't it?"

"Esther!" Miss Osbourne said in a reprimanding voice.

Jack couldn't help but chuckle. "You are quite right, Miss Osbourne. I also like to think of my club as a refuge from chaotic family life."

"Oh, yes," Esther said. "Do you have a family, Mr. Corbin?"

"No. I don't."

"Oh," she said in a sad voice.

"Mr. Corbin is also in charge of the finances for the railroad that will soon pass through Willowbrook," Miss Osbourne added.

"Oh my. That is quite an undertaking."

"Yes, it is. It's also the reason I came to see your sister," Jack said.

Esther's eyebrows lifted. "Have you come to offer her a position?"

"Yes, I have, but she has not accepted my offer yet."

"Whyever not, Lena?" she asked her sister in a firm voice. "You know it's only a matter of time until the church asks us to leave here. We'll have to look for someplace else to live. We might as well do it now."

"They have already come to see me about leaving," Lena said in a soft whisper.

"Is that who was here earlier?"

"Yes, Essie."

Esther turned her head and faced him directly. "What are you going to offer my sister?"

"I intend to offer her a generous monthly wage and a house where the two of you can live in comfort."

"And what services will she be required to provide to you?"

"Essie!"

"Well, Lena, it's best you get everything out in the open and up front from the beginning."

"Your sister is quite right, Miss Osbourne." Jack turned his attention to Esther, even though he was quite sure she couldn't see him, then cleared his throat. "I have asked your sister to take charge of the accounts and ledgers for the club. I will have to devote my time and efforts to taking care of the railroad accounts and making sure the supplies and materials they require are delivered in a timely manner."

"That will be quite time consuming, Mr. Corbin."

"Which is why I need your sister's assistance."

"You must have heard how knowledgeable she is," Esther said. "She is brilliant with numbers."

"That's what I have heard," Jack said with a smile.

"Not brilliant," Lena said. "Numbers just come easily to me."

"Then you are exactly what I need."

"So, why haven't you given Mr. Corbin an answer yet?" Esther asked. "Were you waiting to see what I would think?"

"Actually, yes," Lena replied.

"Well, I will give you the same answer that Papa would give you if he were here. He would tell you that your choice is between using the gifts God gave you to earn a living, or you can continue to sell buns on the street corner, and we can go hungry."

"What about you, Essie? Who will stay with you?"

"What about Mattie? Can we convince her to spend more time with me every day?"

"Perhaps, but she has a husband to cook for."

"Maybe I can help with this," Jack said. "It would be worth it for me to pay Mattie. Would she agree to stay with you more hours for a handsome wage?"

"You would cover the cost of Mattie's wages?" Esther asked.

"It would be worth it to me in the long run," Jack said.

"I will discuss it with her, then," Lena said.

"Do you have any more questions?" Jack asked.

"What about our living quarters?" Esther asked. "Is it a cottage that we could rent?"

"No, no. I will provide a home for you and your sister. Now," he said, knowing that he'd accomplished the opposite of what he'd originally intended, "do you have any other questions?"

"No," both ladies responded.

"Perhaps something will come up later that we need to discuss, but for now I think we've covered everything," Esther added.

Jack reached out, took Esther's hand, and brought her fingers to his lips. "It was a pleasure to meet you, Miss Osbourne."

"It was a pleasure to meet you too, Mr. Corbin. Thank you for coming."

"My pleasure."

Lena stood and turned. "I'll be back in a moment, Essie," she said, then took Jack's arm and walked with him back to the house.

"Thank you," she said when they were inside.

"For what?"

"For treating Esther as if she were a normal woman instead of different from everyone else."

"She *is* a normal woman. She just can't see."

"You would be amazed at the number of people who think because she cannot see, nor can she think, or hear, or understand common thoughts or words."

"It's obvious that she is a very intelligent woman. And I believe that because of you, she has developed her intelligence far beyond what is normal for someone without sight."

"She has a hunger for the written word," Lena said. "I read to her as often as I can. She devours books."

"I don't doubt that. I'll make sure I don't keep you so busy that you don't have time to read to her."

"I would appreciate that, sir. Thank you."

"I think I'm the one who owes you a debt of gratitude, Miss Osbourne. You have taken a great deal of pressure off my shoulders. I think we will make good partners. I look forward to working with you."

Jack bade her good day and left the cottage. He was elated at how this day had gone, and yet it hadn't gone at all like he'd anticipated it would. Or how he had wanted it to go.

He'd told himself he wouldn't hire a woman under any circumstances. Yet that was exactly what he'd done.

He'd told himself that he wouldn't be influenced by a pretty face, or a female who needed to be rescued. Yet that was exactly what he'd done.

He wondered what he was getting himself into.

CHAPTER FOUR

"ESSIE, COME HERE. Mr. Corbin will be here any minute now."

"Are you excited, Lena?" Essie said, coming around the corner.

"A bit, yes. We've never lived anyplace but here in the parsonage. This will be a new beginning for the both of us."

"What is he like?"

"Who? Mr. Corbin?"

"Yes."

"Well, he's quite tall, and he has a presence about him that exudes strength and leadership. He has a pleasant personality, and when he speaks, he commands attention."

"But what does he look like?"

"Oh," Lena said.

"Is he handsome?"

Lena had a difficult time answering that question.

"Well, is he?" Essie asked.

"He is probably the most handsome man I have ever seen in my life."

"Oh," Essie said with a giggle. "Does he have glorious hair?"

"Oh yes. And lots of it."

"And his eyes?"

"Large and penetrating...and a bit merry, too, I think. Blue like the blue of the sky after a thunderstorm."

"And his smile? Does he smile often?"

"I have not been around him enough to know if he smiles often, but when he does smile, it seems to bring the daylight right indoors."

"Oh, Lena. He sounds divine," Essie gushed.

"Silly girl, of course he sounds divine. I could describe a troll and you would think he sounded divine."

"Of course I would."

"Oh, here he is. Do you have a shawl?"

"Do you think I need one?"

"No, the weather is perfect. You shouldn't need one, I suppose."

Lena took Essie's arm and led her from the cottage. They reached the edge of the walk just as the carriage stopped and two men descended.

"Misses Osbourne," Mr. Corbin greeted them. "Allow me to present my partner and friend, Mr. Bradford Prescott. Brad and I served together in the war and became fast friends."

Lena and Essie greeted Mr. Corbin's friend as he helped them into the carriage.

"Are you ready to see your new home?" Mr. Prescott asked when they were seated in the carriage.

"Yes," Essie said, holding on to Lena's hand. "Lena just reminded me that we haven't lived anywhere but the parsonage, so this will be a grand adventure."

"You'll think so when you have to help me clean our new house," Lena added. "It is bound to be bigger than the tiny parsonage we just left."

Mr. Corbin laughed. "I promise it's quite a bit larger than the parsonage, but you won't have to bother with any cleaning. The house comes with its own staff. All you'll have to worry about is telling them what to do and they will do it."

Essie looked at Lena with a stunned expression. "We will have our own maid?" she asked.

Mr. Corbin smiled, and so did his friend. "Miss Osbourne, you will have several maids and footmen, a cook, a butler, and gardeners to care for the parks."

"Oh," Lena said softly. Suddenly, this was all too much, and it seemed as if she were Mr. Corbin's kept woman instead of his employee.

"What is wrong?" he asked.

"Your house sounds too grand, Mr. Corbin. My sister and I are not accustomed to living in luxury. We have never had much, nor do we expect much. We will be quite comfortable living in a small cottage."

"I'm afraid you will have to get used to more luxurious accommodations, Miss Osbourne. Besides, you will no doubt be so busy you will not have time to clean and cook and do all the things you used to do before. At least, not if you want time to be with your sister and read, as you have indicated you are fond of doing."

"I see," Lena said, thinking over the choices before her.

"Why don't we see the house first, then discuss our options?" Mr. Prescott said in a calming voice.

For the first time, Lena concentrated on Mr. Corbin's friend and noticed several things about him. He had a great many scars on his face and hands. It almost seemed as if he had been tortured, and whoever tortured him was an expert at causing pain.

Although very little of his body could be seen, she did notice that almost every exposed part was a mass of old wounds. And it seemed as if some of his flesh had been torn from his body. She shivered at the thought of what he must have endured.

"Are you chilled?" Mr. Corbin asked.

"No. I'm just trying to accustom myself to what might be ahead of us."

He smiled one of his heart-stopping grins. "Much," he said softly. "And we are almost there."

"I have a suggestion, before we arrive," Essie said, interrupting a tense moment.

"And what would that be?" Mr. Prescott asked with a smile.

"My name is Esther, but everyone calls me Essie. I would like it if you do also."

"I would be honored, Essie," Mr. Prescott replied. "And my name is Bradford, but my friends call me Brad."

"You have friends, Brad?" Mr. Corbin said with playful mockery, and everyone laughed. "And while my name is Jackson, my friend calls me Jack."

"You have only *one* friend, Mr. Corbin?" Essie asked.

"Yes, Miss Osbourne. My other acquaintances call me Mr. Corbin or Major, because they are my employees. I pay them quite handsomely to call me Mr. Corbin. And you, Miss Osbourne?" he said, focusing on Lena.

"My name is Magdalena, but my friends, of whom I have several, call me Lena. You may also," she said, "except when I am working. Then you will call me Miss Osbourne."

"Good," Essie exclaimed. "That is settled, and just in time. I think we are almost at our new home."

"How did you know that?" Brad asked in amazement.

"By the speed and the shifting of the carriage," she answered. "Being blind doesn't affect your brain. It only heightens your other senses."

"You are quite remarkable, Essie. Quite," Brad said.

"I wish everyone saw me as that," she said, then readied herself to descend from the carriage.

The horses slowed and stopped, and Jack alighted first while Brad did the same from the opposite side. Jack helped Lena to the ground, and Brad assisted Essie. When they had disembarked, Brad brought Essie around the carriage to stand next to Lena. She reached for her hand, and Lena gripped her fingers tightly.

They stood there in silence while Lena stared at the magnificent house before her.

"What is it, Lena?"

"Oh, Essie. It takes my breath away. It's the most splendid

country home I've ever seen. It's enormous. A mansion. Is this yours?" she asked, turning to Jack.

"Yes," he answered as he led Lena and Essie to the entrance. A butler opened the door before they reached it. "Franklin, this is Miss Magdalena Osbourne and her sister, Miss Esther Osbourne. They will be staying here for the time being."

"Very good, Mr. Corbin. Welcome to Corbin House, ladies."

"Thank you, Franklin," Essie and Lena said in unison.

"Let me show you to your rooms," Jack said, then led the way to a staircase.

"We're in the foyer, Essie," Lena said. "To go upstairs you'll go right about six steps"—Essie did—"then reach out for the banister on your right."

Essie reached out and placed her hand on the railing. "Are there several steps, Lena?"

"I'd say about eighteen. Shall we count them?"

"Yes," Essie answered, then began counting as she took the first step. "That was a good guess," she said when she reached the top on the eighteenth step.

"Yes," Jack said from behind them. "Now, would you like a cup of tea before we go back down?"

"I would love one," Essie said, and Lena agreed with her.

"Franklin, would you ask Cook to send a tea tray to the sitting room?"

"Right away, sir," the butler replied. "And here's Mrs. Franklin. She'll take over until I return."

"Ladies, I'd like you to meet my housekeeper, Mrs. Franklin," Jack said. "She is married to my butler, as you might have guessed by now."

"How do you do?" Lena and Essie greeted her.

"Mrs. Franklin," Jack continued, "this is Miss Magdalena Osbourne." The housekeeper bobbed a polite curtsy. "And her sister, Miss Esther Osbourne." She curtsied again. "If there's anything you need, you have only to ask, and Mrs. Franklin will take care of you."

Lena smiled, and the housekeeper returned it, which was both pleasant and welcoming.

"First," Lena said, "I would ask that you provide my sister with someone she may call upon to help her find her way in the house, until she becomes accustomed to its layout."

"Of course. I think Betsy would be the perfect choice."

"Thank you," Essie said. "I assure you it won't take me long to learn where I'm going, but I have to admit that this is ever so much larger than anything Lena and I are used to."

"You'll learn soon enough," Mrs. Franklin said. "It took all of us time to learn its twists and turns, and we have perfect sight!"

Essie laughed, then turned to Mrs. Franklin. "Thank you," she said. "I'm ever so glad you didn't ignore my blindness. Most people either avoid me or they pretend if I can't see, I probably can't hear, either."

"Well, you won't find that here. We're pleased to have you with us. Now, would you like to see your chambers?"

"Yes, please," Essie replied. Lena let her walk beside Mrs. Franklin so she would know where to go.

"This first bedchamber is yours, Miss Esther. If there's anything you don't have, just let someone know and they'll get it for you."

"Does it have a bed?" Essie asked.

"Oh, yes, miss. A nice, big bed."

"Then it will suit me just fine."

"It even has a cushioned chair right here," Lena said. "It's close to the window, so you can feel the heat from the sun when it comes up in the morning or open the window to get a nice breeze."

"Oh, I've never had anything so grand," Essie said. "Thank you, Mr. Corbin. This is wonderful."

Jack acknowledged her compliment, then turned to Lena. "Would you like to see your room now, Lena?"

"Yes, please." She hadn't been this excited in a long time. "Are you coming with us, Essie?"

"Do you mind if I stay here? I'd like to memorize my room."

"Of course," Lena said. "We'll return shortly."

"I'll be here," Essie replied.

"I'll stay with her," Brad said. "I'll be here if she needs any-thing."

"Thank you," Lena said, thinking how nice it was of him to offer. Not many men would think to be so kind.

Lena walked to the door, but Jack stopped her. "This way," he said, walking across the room to a side door. "This will take you into a small room used by a maid, or as a dressing room."

"Oh," Lena said, stepping into the room. "How convenient."

"And here," he said, opening a further door into a spacious sitting room, "is where the lady of the house used to entertain close friends and family."

"Oh my. It's gorgeous."

Lena ran her fingers across a floral brocade sofa and two matching wing chairs.

"Through this door is your bedroom, Lena."

Lena followed him through the door and entered the room that would be hers. She paused and looked around when she entered. "Oh, Mr. Corbin, this is beautiful," she said, placing her hands over her mouth to stop a cry from escaping. "Ever so grand."

"I knew you would like it," he said.

"Was this your room?"

He smiled. "No, I'm afraid the décor is a bit too feminine for my taste. I slept in a room in the other wing, but as long as you and your sister are here, I will sleep at the club. I have rooms there. Because I spend so much time there, it's often easier just to stay there rather than come here."

Lena stepped into the room and took note of the paper on the walls and the furniture. "I see what you mean," she said, touching her fingers to the wallpaper's floral shades of rose, gray, and white. "The colors are just beautiful." Everything in the room was perfect for a lady, from the coordinated bedcovers to the rose-colored basin on the washstand. It clearly was not made for the exceedingly masculine Jackson Corbin.

Just then, Franklin announced that the staff had delivered a tea tray to the sitting room, and Esther and Brad were already there.

"Thank you, Franklin," Jack replied. "I'll show Miss Osbourne in. That will be all."

"Very good, sir," Franklin said, leaving them.

Jack extended his arm, and Lena took it. She knew she would have a reaction to Jack's touch similar to the last time she had inadvertently brushed against him. But she wasn't expecting the warmth that shot up her arm to be as strong as it was. The effect was almost overpowering.

She wondered if he experienced the same intense reaction. She doubted he did. Men did not have the same feelings as women.

She entered the room on his arm, then poured tea for everyone and served a charming plate of pastries. The four of them chatted for a time before Jack gave them a quick tour of the ground floor of the house.

Lena had never seen a home so lovely as Corbin House. Nor had she imagined that she and Essie would ever live in a house so grand. She considered herself one of the luckiest people on earth.

>>>>><<<<<

WHEN THEY FINISHED, they returned to their small cottage.

"Can you believe we'd ever live in a mansion so grand, Lena?" Essie asked, sitting at the kitchen table. "I could walk a full ten paces and not bump into a single thing."

"Never," Lena answered. "Nor did I ever think we'd have a staff of servants to wait on us."

"What do you think Mama and Papa would say?"

Lena propped her elbows on the table and rested her chin in

her palms. "I think that both of them would warn us not to become spoiled with our newfound good fortune. Where we live and what we have doesn't make us different, or better than the least among us."

"You are right, Lena. And we can never forget that."

"Yes. Now, I'll go in the closet and bring out Papa's trunk and we can start packing."

"Very well," Essie said. "I don't imagine it will take us long."

Lena agreed. They had so few personal possessions, it wouldn't take them long at all.

CHAPTER FIVE

LENA SPENT THE next two days packing and cleaning the cottage for their move to Jack's mansion. She'd never thought she and Essie would ever live in a home so grand or luxurious. She wondered what their mother and father would think of living in a home that had servants to wait on them, clean their home, and cook.

But more thought-consuming was what her parents would think of her working at a gentlemen's club. This was something that worried her nearly every hour of the day. And yet, what choice did she have? She had no other option that would enable her to earn a living for herself and Essie.

"Here, Essie," she said, carrying another armload of clothes to where her sister sat in the bedroom they shared. "How are you doing?"

"Fine," Essie said with a smile. She folded and packed everything that they needed to take with them. "Does it look all right?"

"It looks perfect. As long as you put it in the trunk, we'll find it when we unpack."

"Is Mr. Corbin coming today, do you think?"

"Yes," Lena answered. "He said he'd come for me this morning. He wanted me to see his club when there were only a few people there so I would get a feel for what it was like before it became too busy."

"Are you nervous, Lena?"

"Not nervous so much as worried." Lena sat beside Essie on the bed and reached for her hands. "Am I doing the right thing, Essie? Do you think Mama and Papa would approve of my working for Mr. Corbin?"

"I think Mama and Papa would both like Mr. Corbin very much. He is kind and polite, and as nice as any gentleman we've ever met. And I know Papa would have made the same choice you did. He would do everything he could to take care of his family, including keeping books for Jackson's Gentlemen's Club."

"Oh, I hope you are correct."

"I'm sure I am. Now, bring me more clothes to fold so we're ready to leave when Mr. Corbin's men come for our things."

Lena leaned over and kissed her sister's cheek. She would do anything in her power to take care of Essie. Anything.

Lena left the room, took more personal items from what had been their parents' room, and carried them back to Essie. As she set them down, there was a firm knock on the door.

"Do you think that's Mr. Corbin?" Essie asked.

"Yes," Lena answered. "He said he'd be here this morning. I'll tell Mattie where I'm going. She said she'd be here with you."

"Good luck," Essie said, and smiled as Lena left the room.

Lena walked to the door and opened it. Jack stood before her, and her heart shifted in her breast. Why did he have such an effect on her? Just the sight of him caused her heart to beat faster.

"Good morning, Mr. Corbin. Please, come in."

It wasn't until he entered the house that she noticed he wasn't alone. Brad was with him.

"Mr. Prescott," she greeted him. "Please, come in."

"Miss Osbourne. I hope you don't mind. I came to see if I might be of some use to your sister."

"How kind of you. I'm sure she will welcome your help."

"She isn't alone, is she?"

Lena shook her head. "No, Mattie is here. Thank you for paying her wages, Mr. Corbin. I don't know how I can ever repay you for everything you are doing for us."

A broad smile crossed his face. "You'll know soon enough when you see the amount of work I intend to heap upon you."

Lena matched his smile. "I look forward to it." Her gaze remained locked with his, and Lena felt the connection between them growing. She couldn't allow her emotions to shift in that direction. Her connection to Jack Corbin was intensifying, and she dared not allow that to happen.

She broke their contact and shifted her attention to Brad. "Let me take you to Essie. She'll tell you how you can help her. Then I'll go to the kitchen and tell Mattie I'm leaving. If you need anything, just call for Mattie."

"I will," Brad said, then followed her to where Essie still sat folding clothes and putting things in the trunk.

"Haven't you gone yet, Lena?" she asked.

"No, Essie. I brought someone to help you."

"Oh?"

"Hello, Miss Osbourne."

"Mr. Prescott," she greeted him with a bright smile lighting her face.

Lena smiled at the look her sister shared with Brad and got a warm feeling. He was a special young man, and her sister realized it.

"I'm going now. You can work for a bit, then take Mr. Prescott to the kitchen and have Mattie give you a cup of tea and a pastry."

Lena blanched at her own words. She'd issued instructions and permissions as if her sister was a mere child, not a woman capable of showing Mr. Prescott simple courtesies. But Essie didn't appear to mind.

"Yes, Lena," she said.

Lena left them and returned to where Jack was waiting near the front door.

"Are you ready?" he asked.

"Yes. And very anxious to see what I'm getting myself into."

"I think you'll be very impressed," he said, escorting her to his waiting carriage and assisting her inside. "It's turned into a very popular place for the gentlemen of Willowbrook to gather, and because of the admittance fee, only those with money can afford to belong or to gamble."

Lena looked at the fellow. He seemed pleased at what he'd just said, but to her mind, catering to men of extravagant means—and excluding those less fortunate—might not necessarily be the most honorable endeavor. That, in a nutshell, was the thing that worried her.

One of the things, at any rate.

After a brief, jolting ride, the carriage turned a corner and traveled down a narrow alleyway.

"This will take you to a private entrance that only three people have keys to enter: myself, Brad, and now you."

When the carriage stopped, he reached into his pocket and handed her a key. Lena looked at the oddly shaped metal object and frowned.

"It's a one-of-a-kind key," he explained, "specially designed so that it cannot be duplicated. Come," he said, stepping out of the carriage and helping her to the ground. "Let me show you how it works."

He led her to the door and lifted a lid that covered a keyhole. "Now, insert the key and turn it to the left."

"The left?" she asked, knowing that was backward from other keys.

"Yes, the left."

She did as he said and heard a loud click.

"Now pull on the door."

Lena pulled the door open and entered. She heard another click when the door closed.

"Stop," he ordered her.

Lena stopped.

"The door locked behind you," he said. "No one can get in with you. You are completely safe."

"I see you have taken every precaution," Lena said, lifting her gaze to meet his.

"My safety and that of my employees is very important," Jack replied. "Perhaps it's because of my experience during the war, or perhaps I'm just overly cautious. Whatever it is, safety is paramount."

"Is that where Mr. Prescott got his injuries? In the war?"

Jack's features turned dark. "Yes. He was captured by the Russians and tortured. I am surprised he's been as open with you and your sister as he has been. He usually avoids being around people."

"Perhaps he feels more comfortable because he knows Essie cannot see his scars."

"I imagine so. He has missed female company since that day, and finally has someone he can be around who doesn't see his deformities and isn't frightened of him."

"Were you captured, too?" she asked.

"I was," he answered, then turned away from her.

It was obvious that he didn't want to talk about it.

"Come, let me show you your office."

"Yes, of course."

Lena walked a half step behind and studied the serious expression on his face. His jaw was set, the muscle in his cheek pulsing. Someday she would have to ask him about his experience in the war. But not today.

The hall was more than an employees' entrance, with fine-quality tiles dressing the ceiling, and rather elegant gas sconces set high on the walls. Lena couldn't help but notice that they were placed properly to sweep the carpeted walkway with even light. It seemed nothing had been spared in making this a place where gentlemen of means would find themselves right at home.

"There are three rooms along this hallway. The first one is mine. The second will be yours. And the third office is Brad's." They walked past the first room with its engraved brass plate designating Jack's office and entered the door beyond. "This room was used mostly for storage, but I added a desk and extra lighting. I hope it will be adequate for your office."

Lena looked around the room and smiled. "This is perfect," she said. The room was spacious, with more-than-adequate lighting. A large desk stood in the center of the room, with three wooden cabinets flanking it on the far wall. It seemed odd, though, that there were three large, round windows on the inner wall. Lena stepped closer.

"These are most unusual," she remarked as she stepped toward the windowed wall.

Jack stepped up beside her. "We call these our spyglasses. Come closer and look. See how the glass is angled?"

Lena did as he suggested and gasped. Once she stood near enough to the large center porthole—which was what to her mind they seemed to be—the glassy haze cleared and the gambling den below came into view. Only it seemed closer than it ought to. Somehow magnified.

She turned her startled gaze to meet the smile on his face.

"I can see the… How did you…? Can they see me?"

"All they see from the gambling floor are three pretty gold globes, but inside each globe is a series of magnifying mirrors that give me this perfect bird's-eye view of everything going on down there. They can't see you, nor anyone in this room. It's the best way for me to see what's going on in my club. I can stop trouble before it gets out of hand."

"Oh, I see. I had no idea such a…a device existed."

Jack laughed. "It does now, although it didn't before Brad stumbled onto the idea." He leaned close and lowered his voice. "It's our secret, Miss Osborne, so please don't reveal it to anyone. In fact, if someone other than you will be in the room, it's a good idea to draw these curtains before they enter." He reached for a tasseled cord and drew an elegant velvet drape across the three portholes. Or spyglasses, as her employer had called them. "It's our best defense against cheating, you see. Sometimes our only defense. But there's no need for anyone to know about Brad's invention."

"What do you do if you spot someone cheating?"

"I ask them to leave and tell them not to come back."

"Oh," Lena said as she watched several men playing cards down below, even though it was early in the day.

"Brad usually helps me watch the players, but as you know, he is more interested in your sister than watching for cheaters at the moment."

Lena lifted her gaze and met Jack's smile. "Yes, so it seems."

She watched the activity a few moments more, then went to her desk and sat. Jack followed her and sat in a chair in front of her desk.

"What exactly will be my routine?" she asked.

"This is the ledger you will work from." He stood and opened the book before her. "You can see where I left off."

Lena studied the page in front of her. From the top to almost the middle of the page, it was filled with Jack's writing. His numbers were bold, and showed a strength that matched his personality. There was nothing weak in his writing.

"Every morning when you arrive, you will find this metal box on your desk. Here is the key that will open it." He handed her another key.

Lena opened the padlock and lifted the lid to the box. She looked inside and sat back in shock. Inside were several bags of money.

"There are nine gambling stations on the floor. Each bag is numbered according to the station it came from. As you see here, this came from table one. That's the front table on the right. It's usually a poker table. Table two is another poker table. You can learn more about each table later. Just know that each page is numbered according to the table it represents.

"When you come in each morning, you will divide the bags according to the tables they came from. Then, starting with the bags from table one, you will count out the money and enter the sums on the correct pages."

Lena listened while Jack explained the procedure. When he finished, he looked at her and smiled.

"Any questions?"

"Of course. I have several questions, but I won't know exactly what to ask until I go through the procedure the first time."

Jack studied her confused expression several seconds before he laughed. "I don't expect you to understand what you are doing for a week or two."

"Or three," she added on a sigh.

"Or more," he added.

"Hopefully, it won't take me that long. If it does, you'll lose all faith in my abilities."

"No, I won't do that," he said, shaking his head. "But do you have any questions right now?"

"One that I can think of. What time do you expect me to arrive each morning?" she asked.

"That is up to you. If you feel more comfortable working early, come early. If you would rather stay home with Essie, then do that. Your hours are your own, although you'll find it will be best to begin by noon so that you complete your work before the bank closes every day. Lock the money in the box and stack the bags according to table on that wooden tray." He pointed to a large maple tray poised on the right edge of her desk. "It's Brad's job to get the bags back to the tables and the money to the bank or into the safe." He smiled. "Oh! And you should know that there are two complete sets of bags, so one set is always at the tables, and the other should be here with you. All right?"

Lena nodded.

"Don't worry," he said, taking her hand. "I will, of course, work with you for the first several days, or until you catch on to what you are doing."

Lena looked down to where his hand was atop hers. His flesh was sending a wave of heat that traveled up her arm and wrapped around her heart.

She slowly lifted her head. She wasn't sure why he affected

her like he did, but the emotions that surged through her were too confusing for her to decipher.

"U-um…" she stammered. "Do you want to help me enter this day into the ledger?"

"Well…why…why don't you start by counting out the money for table one? I…I need to get a cup of coffee. I'll be right back," he said, and left the room.

Lena sat back in her chair the moment the door closed behind him.

What on earth had just happened? She wasn't worried that she wouldn't be able to understand the job he expected her to do. But she was terrified that she wouldn't be able to protect herself if she had to spend several hours every day with Jackson Corbin. She was already in jeopardy of losing her heart. Something she couldn't risk doing. It would only lead to heartache and disappointment.

Her first responsibility was to Essie. No one could come before her sister, and Jack didn't seem the type of man who would be satisfied being second in any relationship.

CHAPTER SIX

FOR THE HUNDREDTH time, Jack told himself that hiring Lena to work with him was the biggest mistake he'd ever made. It was all he could do to sit beside her while he instructed her on how to keep the ledgers. He wanted to touch her so desperately that his hands ached with desire. He wanted to kiss her so badly that it was all he could do to keep from leaning close to her and pressing his lips to hers.

The desire he felt was nearly torture. In the mere two days she'd worked for him, he'd lost count of the number of times he'd fled her office on some flimsy excuse. It was either that or take her in a crushing embrace.

The fine china coffee cup rattled against its saucer when he set it down. Mother of God, he'd been trembling like a schoolboy. He would either get a grip on his lust or terminate her employment.

Jack swept a hand across his brow. He'd never do that, and he knew it. She had expressed her gratitude so sweetly, so earnestly, that he knew he'd do whatever it took to keep her safe and happy. And working. Now all he had to do was convince himself he was ready to go back into her office and face her again.

"I think I've got all the money counted," she said when he entered, "and the totals entered into the ledger. What's next?"

"Get the money ready to deposit, and I'll take it to the bank."

He handed her the slips she would need and gave her the large leather satchel he used for deposits. The bag locked with a small padlock that only Jack could open, and had a thick leather strap. When the bag was ready, he put the strap over his shoulder and stood.

"Now, I'll take it to the bank."

"Will I do this every day?"

"No," he said more firmly than he intended. "Ordinarily, Brad and I will take it to the bank, but today, I'll get one of the footmen to ride guard."

"Guard?"

"Yes. I always take a guard."

"I can see why," she said. "There's more money in your bag than I've ever seen at one time in my life."

Jack couldn't hide his smile. "Last night was a good night. Not all are that good, but most are close."

"I'm happy for you, Jack. You've clearly worked hard to make your club a success."

"I've had to. I was born into poverty, and my parents both died before I was ten years old. I learned early on that I could either take advantage of what life had to offer, or let it destroy me. I decided I wanted to take advantage of everything I could. Thankfully, I was blessed with a body that made me look older than I was. When I was just fifteen, I looked like I was twenty. I got a job working in a men's club in London."

"Is that when you decided you wanted to own your own club?"

He smiled again. "Yes. All I saw was money being spent by London's titled, and I realized owning my own club was how I was going to make it in the world. Unfortunately—or perhaps fortunately—I suffered from a wave of patriotism. I joined Her Majesty's army, and that postponed my dream of owning a club."

"What rank did you hold?"

"I rose to the rank of major. That's where I met Brad. He was a lieutenant and was assigned to my platoon. We became fast friends and learned to watch each other's backs. I survived the war because of him."

Jack thought back to those dark days when he and Brad were held hostage and fought the pain that nearly brought him to his knees.

"How did you earn the money to start the club? It must have taken more than you made on a soldier's salary."

"Oh, yes. A great deal more."

Jack opened the bottom drawer of one of the file cabinets and removed a bottle of brandy. He poured a liberal amount into a glass and offered it to her, but Lena refused, which he'd assumed she would.

He sat on the chair next to where she sat and took a sip of his brandy. "I met the Duke of Willowbrook's grandson, the Earl of Murdock, during the war. I told him my goal of running a men's club, and he told me about Willowbrook and said he was willing to loan me enough money to open an establishment. He is the one who set down the ground rules for the club, with which, of course, I gladly complied."

"What were some of those rules?"

"Mainly, he wanted my assurance that the tables would always be honest. He would abide no cheating, and neither would I."

"No one would ever think you would," she said.

"I'm glad you realize that," he said, then took another sip of his brandy. "When Brad and I were released from hospital, we came to Willowbrook. I knew the first time I toured the town that this was where I wanted to settle down. Lord Murdock loaned me the money, and I built Jackson's Gentlemen's Club."

"How wonderful," she said.

Jack finished his brandy, then got to his feet. "I need to take our deposit to the bank," he said. "Will you be all right until I get back?"

"Yes, I'll be fine. I'll double-check my totals while I wait for you."

"It won't take me long," he said, then opened the bottom desk drawer and removed a pistol he kept there. He tucked it into his jacket, then caught the expression on her face. "I've never had to use it," he said by way of explanation, "but it doesn't hurt to have it with me."

"Yes, I can see where it might come in handy. You do have quite a bit of money with you."

"Yes, I do." He anchored the satchel of money over his shoulder and walked to the door. "I won't be gone long," he said, then left the room. He made his way to the front of the club and motioned for George, the man who guarded the door, to come with him.

Jack tried to keep Lena's face from crowding his thoughts and her smile from overtaking his mind, but that didn't happen. She was becoming a part of him, and he couldn't—wouldn't—force her to leave.

LENA WATCHED JACK leave the room and close the door behind him. Just thinking about him made her legs go weak. She sat in the chair behind her desk and tried to get him out of her mind, but that was impossible. She couldn't erase his smile, or the glint in his eyes. Or how her body warmed when he stood close to her. What was wrong with her?

She bolted from her chair and paced the room. She had to get him out of her mind. She had to quit thinking about him and imagining that she could care for him. But she couldn't. It wasn't possible. Her future had been mapped out for her from the day Essie had been born. From the time her parents realized that Essie couldn't see.

She'd promised her mother on her deathbed that she would always take care of Essie. That she would never abandon her. And she could never break that promise.

Lena walked to the front of the room to part the drape and look down over the gambling hall. It was growing late in the afternoon, and the club was becoming more crowded. Nearly half of the tables were busy, and Lena had an unobstructed look at men enjoying themselves with cards, dice, and a wheel that a man in an official Jackson's Gentlemen's Club jacket and red silk ascot dropped a little ball into, letting it go round and round until the wheel stopped and the ball landed in one of the spaces.

The man in a chair on the right side of the table stood up and cheered excitedly, while the man in the red ascot slid several wooden coins to the winner's growing pile.

Lena was so intent on watching the players that she hadn't heard the door open and Jack enter.

"Can you figure out what is going on?" he asked, stepping up beside her.

"Oh!" she squeaked, and Jack laughed.

"I'm sorry," he said, still laughing. "I didn't mean to startle you."

"I was so interested in what was going on below that I didn't hear you."

"What were you watching?"

"What game are they playing on table number five?" she asked. "The game with the big wheel they spin."

"Oh, that's a roulette wheel."

"What's the purpose of the game?"

Jack explained the rules of the game, and Lena listened intently. "In other words, this game requires no skill. Only chance."

"I guess so," Jack replied.

"Then why do people play it, if there's no skill involved?"

"I'm not sure," he answered.

"Do you ever play it?"

"No."

"That's interesting," Lena said, wanting to ask more, but guessing he didn't want to answer. "What do you play?"

"I don't gamble," he said, looking at her as if he needed to see her reaction.

"You don't gamble?"

"No. It's not wise to gamble with the customers."

"I can understand that. They might accuse you of cheating if you won all the time."

"Yes," he replied. "And I never lose."

Lena couldn't hide her surprise. She turned to face Jack. "You *never* lose?" she said on a laugh.

"No." His expression was deadly serious. "I'm not sure why, but it's as if I know what cards my opponents have before we play each hand."

"How is that possible?"

"I don't know. My mind seems able to count the cards played so I know what cards are left. I've always had that curse."

"You call that a curse?"

"It is. I'd love to sit down and play a hand of cards…and lose. Just once."

"Oh my," Lena said, breathing a heavy sigh.

"That is why I consider it a curse." Jack paused. "I am cursed with the same ability when I read something or see something. I can recall what I see or read without writing it down. It came in quite handy during the war, until I was caught looking at secret files."

"Is that when you were imprisoned and tortured?"

"Yes. The Russians didn't believe me when I told them that I hadn't taken anything, even though they couldn't find that anything had been stolen."

"Oh," she said.

"Enough about me, though. Are you ready to go home? I imagine your sister is more than ready to get rid of her visitor and have some peace and quiet."

Lena laughed as she collected her cape, and Jack helped her put it on. "I doubt that. Essie gets visitors so seldom, I'm sure it's your friend Brad who is more than ready to escape."

Jack showed Lena how to lock her office, then escorted her to his waiting carriage.

"This is George, Miss Osbourne. George, this is Miss Osbourne."

Lena greeted the man who was waiting to escort them. When Lena and Jack were both inside the carriage, the carriage took off toward Corbin House.

"It will be interesting to see who is more in need of being rescued, your sister or my friend," he said when the carriage stopped in front of the house. "Would you like to wager?"

"I wager it is your friend," Lena said as they walked to the front door.

"And I wager it is your sister," Jack replied as they entered the house.

They stepped into the foyer and stopped short.

"Do you hear that?" Jack said with a frown.

"I do," Lena answered. "I think it's coming from the kitchen."

"It is," Jack said, pausing to listen to the riotous laughter coming from another part of the house.

He tucked Lena's hand under his arm and escorted her to the other end of the house. They entered the kitchen and stopped.

Essie and Brad, along with Cook and one of the younger footmen, were seated at the table with a crowd of servants gathered around them.

"Who is that man sitting beside my sister?" Lena asked.

"He's one of my stable hands," Jack answered. "He takes care of the horses."

"What are they doing?"

"It appears that they are gambling," Jack said.

"My *sister* is gambling?"

"I would say so."

"But she can't see."

"Which explains what my stable hand is doing. He is obviously seeing for her."

At that moment, the stable hand lifted the card that Essie should play, and Lena's sister pulled it from the cards in her hand

and slapped it down on the table with a great deal of confidence.

The crowd around the table leaned in to get a look at the card Essie played, then reacted with much clapping and cheering.

Lena focused on her sister and saw the look of pure joy and excitement on her face. She was happier than Lena had ever seen her.

"Who won?" Jack asked, stepping into the room. His voice was firm and commanding, and everyone in the room started in surprise. Lena followed him as he stopped near the table.

"I did," Essie said. The excitement in her voice was evident for all to hear. "Are you home, too, Lena?"

"Yes, Essie. I'm here."

"I won, Lena." She placed her hand on the shoulder of the man sitting next to her. "Didn't I, Rupert? I won, didn't I?"

"Yes, Miss Osbourne. You won," Rupert replied.

"I won two times, didn't I, Brad?"

"You surely did, Essie. You're becoming a regular card sharp," Brad answered, looking at her with a sense of pride.

"That's wonderful, Miss Osbourne, but why don't we all go back to work now?" Jack said in a firm voice. "Cook needs to get dinner started, or we'll all go without eating tonight."

Everyone scrambled from the room and went back to their positions. Lena felt Jack's hand on her back as he led her out of the room, followed by Essie and Brad. He took her to the nearest salon, the one he called the blue room, and showed her to the sofa. He waited until Brad and Essie were seated, then he sat beside her.

Lena studied his face to determine if he was angry but couldn't decide. Before she could ask him, he sat back against the sofa cushions and released a deep, rich laugh. She and Brad released a sigh of relief.

"I don't believe what I just saw," he said when he stopped laughing. "Not only do I own a gaming club in town, but it seems I have one operating in my own home. Did you enjoy learning to play cards, Essie?"

"Oh," Essie said with such excitement that she nearly jumped from her place on the sofa. "I had the best day ever! Do you know what I did before we played cards, Lena?"

"I'm almost afraid to ask," Lena said with tears filling her eyes. She'd never seen Essie so happy, and her heart wanted to burst in her breast.

"Brad and Rupert taught me how to ride!"

"Ride? A horse?"

"Yes! And it was marvelous. Simply marvelous. It was almost like flying."

Lena turned her head and stared at Jack. The smile he shared with her stopped her from breathing.

"I think Brad has ruined your sister forever, Lena."

"If you had seen how much your sister enjoyed herself," Brad said, "you wouldn't think she ruined herself. I think she *found* herself. She has more courage and zest for life that anyone I've ever met before."

"Aren't you happy for me, Lena?" Essie asked.

Lena leaned over and hugged her sister. "I couldn't be happier. I owe Mr. Prescott a great debt."

"So do I," Essie said, and the look on her face told Lena that Essie had experienced a great deal more today than just learning to play cards and ride a horse. She'd obviously awakened several emotions she never knew existed within her.

CHAPTER SEVEN

JACK HAD GIVEN instructions for Cook to prepare dinner, and when they finished eating, Brad excused himself, saying that he had to return to the club. It was common for Jack to work during the day, and Brad to work at night. It wasn't unusual for Jack to be called in during the days to order supplies and see to business matters, so they decided early on that he might as well work the days, and take the nights off. Even though that seldom happened. More often than not, Jack ended up working day *and* night. In fact, he seemed to prefer it that way.

After Brad left, Lena took Essie to her room and handed her over to Betsy to help her get ready for bed. Then Lena returned to the blue room, where Jack waited for her.

"Did you get your sister settled?" he asked when Lena was seated.

"I did. She had such an exciting day, I think she might sleep until noon tomorrow."

"I'm happy for her," Jack said, reaching for her hand. "And I'm happy for Brad, too."

"Yes," Lena said. "He seemed to have had a good time, too."

She kept her gaze focused on Jack, and the air surrounding them seemed to heat several degrees. "Would you like to walk in the garden before it gets too dark?" she asked.

"I'd love to."

Jack kept her hand in his as he rose and took her to the nearest set of glass-paned doors that led to the garden. From there, he led her across a wide terrace that spanned the length of the back side of the manor house. Across from the doors leading from the blue room was a set of stone steps that led to the garden. They descended the three steps and walked down a pebbled path.

"It's so peaceful here I could sit for hours and do nothing," Lena said, keeping her arm tucked in Jack's elbow. She breathed a deep sigh as he led her to a bench on the edge of the path that overlooked a pond. There were several ducks swimming smoothly in the tranquil water.

"Are you comfortable with the work we need from you?" he asked after a few moments of silence.

"Oh yes," she answered. "You've explained it quite well."

"If you need more time to get settled—"

"No, no, I don't need more time. I know you're working tirelessly on the accounts for the railroad as well as the club. I need to do what I was hired to do."

"What time do you plan to come to work in the morning?" he asked.

"I should be at the club by nine o'clock. Is that soon enough, or would you like me there earlier?"

"No, nine o'clock is fine. I just want to tell my driver what time to be here to pick you up."

"That's not necessary, Jack. Your house is not that far from the club. I can walk it easily."

"No, you won't walk. I don't ever want you to walk to the club, or from the club when you go home. Promise me that you won't."

Lena looked up and caught the serious expression on his face. "Very well. I will wait for your driver to arrive."

"Good."

"Is there a reason you're so protective of me?"

"I would be protective of anyone who does the work you do for me."

Lena frowned. "I don't understand."

"No one knows that you work here yet, or what your job is. Eventually, that will change, though. Once they do, there are unscrupulous people who might decide they can use you to get to me."

"You mean *kidnap* me and demand a ransom for my release?"

"That's exactly what I mean. That's why I want you to go back and forth to work in a carriage. So you will never be alone."

"Has that ever happened to anyone?"

"No, but I don't want to chance that it might."

"You were a good army officer, weren't you?"

He smiled. "That's a change of topics. What makes you think that?"

"You don't just react to things that have already happened. You anticipate what could happen and make plans to prevent such happenings."

"That's what any good officer does when he's responsible for the lives of countless men."

"Your men were lucky to have you," she said, and he draped his arm around her shoulders and brought her closer to him. Lena turned enough in his arms that they faced each other.

Jack was going to kiss her. She knew he was, just as she knew she should move away from him to prevent him from doing so. She was attracted to him more than she should have allowed herself to be, but she couldn't help herself.

She had never met anyone like him. Never had the feelings inside her awakened like Jack was able to do. She couldn't allow herself to acknowledge those feelings. She'd known that from the day she faced the fact that Esther wasn't the only one affected by her blindness. Lena was, too.

She had always taken care of her sister. And she couldn't do that if she allowed herself to fall in love with someone. No man would want a wife who could only give him half her love, half her time, half her heart. He would want all her heart. A marriage was between a man and a woman. Not between a man and a woman and another woman.

Not that marriage had even entered Jack's mind. Nor had it hers. Their relationship was far, far, far from that, which was why it was imperative that she prevent him from kissing her before it went that far.

And yet...

Lena couldn't help but wonder what it would be like to kiss him. She'd never kissed anyone before, and something inside her wanted to know. Not that she wanted to know what kissing anyone would be like. Just what kissing *Jack* would be like. But she couldn't.

Lena struggled with her emotions, but before she could steel her determination, Jack lowered his head and pressed his lips to hers.

It was as if time froze. With his lips covering hers, Lena gave in to her raging emotions. Jack's kiss caused the most startling feelings to surge through her. A warmth that turned to an intense heat consumed her.

Every muscle inside her weakened, and her heart thundered in her breast as if it were running a race. Without urging it to, her body gave in to the emotions Jack created within her.

For some reason she couldn't explain, she wanted more from him. She skimmed her hands up his chest, then wrapped her arms around his neck and held him close to her.

From somewhere in the distance, a small whimper escaped, and Lena realized that whimper had come from her. It was a plea. Not a request, but a demand.

As if he understood her need, Jack deepened his kiss. He gave her what she was desperate to have, even though she wasn't sure what that was.

He kissed her again and again, and Lena accepted each kiss as if it contained the air she needed to breathe. She'd never experienced anything like this, had no idea a man's kiss could cause her body to react with such desperation.

He took her once more in a kiss that was tender and all-consuming, then he slowly lifted his mouth from hers and brought her to him, as if he knew she needed his strength to remain upright.

Thankfully, Jack held her close, or Lena was certain that she would have crumpled to the ground.

"We shouldn't have done that," he whispered softly enough that she knew he didn't intend for her to hear him, but she did.

"I'm sorry my kiss was a disappointment," she said softly. "I've never kissed anyone before."

"Your kiss was not a disappointment. In fact, it was anything but. It was the most passionate kiss I've ever experienced. That's what was wrong with it. It was so perfect that I want to kiss you again and again." He leaned closer to her and, indeed, kissed her again. "I don't know how I'll ever be able to stop."

"You have to, Jack. We can't continue this."

"I know," he said, releasing her. He stood and stepped away. "I'm sorry, Lena. I'm no good for you. I'm not the kind of man you want or need."

"You're exactly the kind of man I want, but I can't be the woman you need. I come with too many responsibilities." Lena stepped to where Jack stood. "We need to go back in now. Tomorrow will be a long day."

"Yes," he replied, and held out his arm for her to take.

Lena looped her hand through his arm, and they walked down the same path to the terrace. When they reached the foyer, Jack opened the door to the house and stepped out into the darkness.

"I'll have the carriage out front tomorrow morning."

"Thank you," Lena said. "And we'll forget tonight ever happened."

"Yes," he said as he turned away. "We'll forget this night ever happened. As well as the kiss."

LENA ROSE EARLY the next morning and readied herself to go to work. She hadn't planned to start her day so early, but after the kiss she'd shared with Jack last night, she had been unable to go to sleep.

She hadn't exactly planned on going to work her first day with no sleep, but no matter how hard she tried, it had been impossible. She couldn't stop thinking about the kiss they'd shared.

Lena pressed her fingers to her lips and held them there. It was as if she could pretend he was still with her, that he still kissed her.

She dropped her fingers from her lips and left her room. She wanted to tell Essie goodbye and make sure she had everything she needed for the day. She also wanted to tell her sister that she wasn't sure what time she would be home, but someone would be with her, either Mattie or Betsy.

Essie was fine with that arrangement—in fact, she told Lena that she looked forward to having the day to herself. Brad had chosen a book to read to her yesterday, and she was going to ask whoever was with her today to continue reading to her.

Lena kissed her sister goodbye, then went down to the kitchen to get the lunch Cook had promised to pack for her, as well as a jar with something to drink. When she had everything she needed, she went to the foyer to wait for the carriage Jack had promised to send.

She didn't have to wait long. The carriage pulled up in front of the manor house, and Lena went out to go to her first real day at work.

She removed the key from her reticule and followed the instructions Jack had given her, and within minutes she was inside the office he'd shown her. Jack was waiting for her.

"Did you have any trouble?" he asked.

"No. Everything worked just as it was supposed to."

"Good." He walked to her desk and pointed to the box that contained the money from the day before. "I haven't done anything with it yet. I wanted you to be the only one who touched it."

"Thank you. I appreciate that."

"So," he said, sitting in a chair next to her desk and lifting the cup of coffee he'd been drinking. "What are you going to do first?"

"I'm going to count each table's money and get it ready for you and Brad to take to the bank."

"Perfect. Do you want me to stay here while you count the money and put the amounts in the ledger?"

"No," she answered. "That's not necessary. But I would appreciate it if you would check over my work before you take the deposit to the bank."

"I'll be glad to."

He turned to leave her office, but she stopped him. "Jack?"

He turned to face her.

"We made an agreement last night. We said we were going to forget what happened in the garden, but obviously you haven't. You're as nervous as someone who just got caught stealing half of Cook's biscuits from the oven."

She smiled. It took him a moment or two before he could match her expression, but eventually he did. Then he swiped his hand down his face in embarrassment and laughed.

"I didn't sleep well last night."

"Neither did I," she said.

"I regret kissing you. It put our feelings for each other on a different level."

"I know," she replied. "I'm not sure I can handle that right now."

He nodded his agreement. "Today will be better," he said in a voice that contained little confidence.

"Yes. Today will be better," she responded in a voice that contained even less confidence.

It promised to be a very long day.

CHAPTER EIGHT

L ENA SURVIVED HER first day working alone. She wasn't sure how, but she remembered the instructions Jack had given her, and managed to accomplish more than she thought she would. She sat back in her chair and shifted her shoulders to ease her stiff back.

"It's time you went home, Lena," Jack said from the doorway. "You've been here long enough."

"I was just going to—"

"Whatever it is, you can do it tomorrow."

Lena relaxed her shoulders and stood. "You're correct. There's always tomorrow."

"You did a great job today. I knew you would, but you accomplished even more than I expected you to."

"So, you don't intend to let me go after the first day?" she said, laughing.

"Absolutely not. I'd just have to train someone new to take over your position."

"Did you manage to make some headway with your work with the railroad expenses?"

"Yes, but I realized it's going to be a much bigger job than I anticipated."

"Perhaps if I get my work done early, there will be something I can do to help you."

"There might be," he said with a smile. "For today, though, you need to go home and catch up on your sleep."

Lena met his smile and took her bonnet and reticule from the cabinet. "I'll see you in the morning," she said, walking through the door Jack held open for her.

"George should have the carriage waiting for you. If ever he's late, stay inside until he arrives."

Lena appreciated how concerned he was for her, but knew his overprotectiveness was misplaced. This was Willowbrook, for heaven's sake. It was one of the safest towns in England.

She walked past Jack with a smile, then went to the back door. George was already waiting for her, but she knew he would be. She walked to the carriage and stepped inside.

"Did you have a good day, miss?" he asked before he closed the door.

"Very good, thank you, George."

"I'm glad. Mr. Corbin is a good employer."

"Yes, he is," she said softly as George climbed atop the carriage and they moved off.

It only took a few minutes to arrive at Corbin House. Lena bade George goodnight and walked to the house.

"Hello, Franklin," she greeted the butler.

"Hello, Miss Osbourne."

"Is my sister close?"

"Yes, Miss Osbourne. She's in the library with Mr. Prescott and Mattie."

"Oh, is Mr. Prescott here?"

"Yes, he's been here for most of the afternoon."

"Thank you, Franklin," she said, then headed to the library.

When Lena reached the room, she stopped at the door. She could hear Brad talking in a deep voice, and after listening for a few seconds, she realized he was reading. Lena opened the door and stepped into the room.

Brad saw her and stopped reading, then stood with a finger keeping his place in the book.

"Don't stop," Essie said, sitting up straighter.

"I have to, Essie. We have company."

"Lena!" she called out. "Is that you?"

"It is. What is Brad reading to you?"

"*The Count of Monte Cristo*," she answered. "You read it to me before, but Brad said he's never read it, so I told him I wanted to hear it again."

"Are you enjoying it?" Lena asked.

"Very much. It's quite exciting," Brad answered.

"I knew you'd like it," Essie said, and smiled at him. He returned her smile even though she couldn't see it.

Brad shifted his gaze to focus on Lena. "How was your day?"

"There's much to learn," Lena admitted, sitting. "I discovered several more things I needed to do in order to keep good records."

"Did Jack help you?"

"Yes, he was a great help. I couldn't have managed without him."

"What surprised and intrigued you the most?"

"Oh, that's an interesting question." Lena thought for a few seconds. "I think what surprised me the most is the amount of money the club takes in from the tables. I didn't realize that men could risk such amounts so cavalierly."

"It is amazing, isn't it?" he asked.

"Yes, but what intrigued me most was the number of men who visited the club. Not the gaming tables, but the number who came to occupy time chatting with other men, or to read the newspapers, or just to conduct business. I didn't realize there was such a need for Jackson's Gentlemen's Club. It made me wonder if a ladies' club would be as successful?"

"What an interesting idea," Brad said. "We might need to consider that someday."

"Yes, that would be interesting. I wonder what Jack would think of that."

"You might be surprised," Brad said as food for thought.

They were silent for a moment, then he closed the book and stood. "It's time I returned to the club. I usually start my shift about this time." He reached for Essie's hand and brought her fingers to his lips. "Thank you for a wonderful afternoon."

"I was the one who had the wonderful afternoon. I so enjoyed your visit. Will I see you tomorrow?"

"Perhaps," he said.

"Oh, I hope so."

"I'll look forward to tomorrow, then," he said, and left.

Lena listened until she heard the outside door close after him before either of them spoke.

"What does he look like, Lena?"

"Mr. Prescott?" she answered, hesitancy in her voice.

"Yes. You know how I can touch a person's face and get an idea of what they look like."

"Yes."

"I tried to touch Brad's face, but he wouldn't let me. He held my hands so I couldn't. What reason could he have for not wanting me to know what he looks like? Is he so terribly ugly?"

"No, Essie. He is not ugly. In fact, I believe that before the war he was quite handsome."

"What happened to him during the war?"

"He and Jack were captured by the enemy and tortured."

Essie's hands flew to her face, and she released a small cry. "Is he scarred?"

"Yes, Essie. Quite severely. He has an ugly scar that runs down the right side of his face from his temple to below his jaw. Jack mentioned that Brad avoids going out in public where ladies are present because of their reaction. It's my opinion that he only feels comfortable around you because you cannot see him."

"I see," Essie whispered. "I never thought I would be glad for my blindness, but if it helps Brad feel comfortable around me, then I am."

Lena reached for Essie's hand and held it. "You are so sweet, Essie. Papa always said God has a purpose for everything He does, and I believe he was right. Perhaps one of your purposes is to be a special friend to Brad and help him be more comfortable around people."

"And perhaps one of Brad's purposes is to be a special friend to me."

"Yes. Perhaps you have both found a special purpose in life. Now," Lena said as she squeezed Essie's hand, "I have asked Cook to prepare an early dinner for us. I have had a tiring day and would like to retire early tonight. Is that all right with you?"

"Of course," Essie said. "Before Franklin calls us for dinner, would you help me choose another book? I think I'll have Betsy read to me for a while after dinner. I don't want to read ahead of where we left off on *The Count of Monte Cristo* so Brad and I remain on the same page."

"That sounds wise."

Lena rose from her chair and went to the shelves. She named several titles, and Essie finally settled on *Gulliver's Travels*. Lena gave her the book, and they talked a few more minutes before Franklin announced that dinner was ready.

Lena ate, then bade Essie good night and went to bed. Surely, she was so tired that she would go right to sleep.

If she could keep from thinking of Jack and the kiss they'd shared the night before.

⇶⥈⥇

THE NEXT DAY and the next went better than the days before. By the end of the second week, Lena almost had her routine down to perfection. She arrived on time, if not a little early, every day and counted out her money, then got it ready for Jack and Brad to take to the bank.

It still bothered her when Jack removed his gun from the bottom drawer of the desk, but she told herself she shouldn't be alarmed. He'd been in the army and was used to firearms.

Growing up in the vicar's parsonage, she was certainly not.

While Jack was gone, Lena entered the amounts from the day before in her ledger, then added all the columns to make sure her totals came out. Usually by the time he and Brad returned, she was ready to put her books away. Then she went to Jack's office and asked if there was anything she could do for him. There always was.

She worked on whatever he wanted her to do, then took a few minutes to watch the action on the floor below. Today she was bothered by some of the day's totals that seemed strange to her, but she was sure she had imagined it.

It was getting late, and Lena was just ready to leave for the day when Jack entered her office.

"Are you still here?" he asked. He carried a glass of brandy into the room and sat in the chair next to her.

"I was almost ready to go home," she said with a tired smile.

"What are you doing?" he asked, pointing to the paper she had in her lap.

"I'm just making notes."

Jack leaned over and glanced at what she had written. A frown creased his forehead. "What is this?" he asked.

"May I ask you a question?"

"Of course."

"Have you ever had any of your dealers take from your club?"

"Are you suggesting that one of my dealers is dishonest?"

Lena closed her eyes. She should have known that he would skip over the possibilities and go right to her accusation. "Perhaps, but I can't be sure."

"I think you'd better tell me where this is coming from." Jack's voice contained a harsh edge, and the expression on his face darkened. "What are you suggesting, Lena?"

"Very well," she said with a sigh. "But I could be wrong. I've only been doing this for a few weeks."

"But you caught on very fast, and you know what you're

doing."

"I just want you to make sure before you take my word at face value."

"I will. I check out anything I hear, regardless of who says it. I always make sure I'm right before I accuse anyone of anything."

Lena sighed again. "Good. There are nine tables below us on the floor."

"Yes," he replied.

"Which table do you think is your most popular table?"

"That would be table one."

"Yes," she agreed. "It's a poker table."

He nodded.

"It's also the table that takes in the most money on a nightly basis. About three weeks ago, the daily take from table one decreased substantially for two nights."

"That could just mean that those were slow nights at the club."

"But they weren't. The nights were in general exceptionally good."

Jack looked down to watch the activity at table one, then sat back in his chair. "Go on."

"I took note of who the dealer was on table one, thinking that the same man would remain on table one, but that wasn't the case. The dealer did not always remain the same."

"No, the dealers rotate throughout the week. Your point being...?"

"I've spent the last three weeks following that particular dealer every night and making note of what table he worked, then comparing the intake of that table."

"What did you find out?"

"His table *always* has several poor nights."

"Stay here," he told her as he rose from his chair. "I want to get Brad."

Jack left the room, then soon returned with Brad. He poured his friend a glass of whiskey, then handed it to him. "Tell Brad what you just told me, Lena."

Lena started her explanation with the same warning she'd given Jack: to verify her accusations before doing anything about them. Then she related the same details that she had told Jack. When she finished, Brad and Jack exchanged serious looks.

"This is the first time we've had a thief in our employ," Brad said.

"That we know of," Jack added.

"Yes, that we know of. So," Brad said before throwing the last of his whiskey to the back of his throat. "What are we going to do about it?"

"We're going to watch his every move to make sure what Lena suspects is true, then we're going to catch him in the act."

Brad nodded, then walked to the window and looked down at the busy floor below. "How does he do it?"

Jack turned to where Lena sat watching the action below. "Do you know, Lena?"

"Not for sure," she answered. "I've been watching him for more than a week now, and I haven't figured it out. All I know is that when he's working, he takes several more breaks than any of the other dealers."

"There he goes," Brad said. "He just motioned for the floor supervisor to step in for him."

Lena looked down to try to follow his movements, but before she could see anything, Brad was out the door and racing to the stairs. He intended to follow the dealer. Lena hoped Brad could see where he went.

When he was gone, she was left alone with Jack. "I hope I'm wrong about your dealer," she said. "I don't want him to be a thief."

Jack looked at her and smiled. "I don't want him to be a thief either, but the world isn't the perfect place we want it to be."

"I know," Lena said, realizing Jack considered her naïve view impossible.

"Now," he said. "You've been here long enough. You need to

get home before Essie accuses me of working you too much and demands that I give you at least one day off on a regular basis."

"Essie knows how busy we are, and how much time it takes to keep the club running, as well as the additional time it takes to make sure the materials are here for the railroad workers when they need them."

"And I know Brad stops in to see her at least once a day," he said with a wink.

"Yes," she replied. "They seem to get along quite well."

"Yes, they do," Jack said, walking her to the door.

He stopped when he reached the door and let his gaze focus on her. Lena wanted him to kiss her, yet knew she shouldn't allow him to take such liberties, especially after what happened the last time she'd let him kiss her. And yet she wanted him to kiss her more than anything.

With their gazes locked, he lowered his head and brought his lips close to hers. A loud knock on the door interrupted them a moment before he kissed her.

Jack lifted his head and turned to the door as it opened.

"Am I interrupting something?"

CHAPTER NINE

JACK DROPPED HIS arms from around Lena and deliberately stepped in front of her. He was desperate to shield her from the new arrival.

"Mr. Barnaby," Jack said in a less-than-welcoming tone. "I wasn't aware that you were coming, or that you had been invited. How did you get past my men?"

Barnaby chuckled. "You have some very suspicious guards, Corbin. I had to practically give them my life's history as to how we were connected in order for them to allow me to see you. My assurance that I was here on your invitation to discuss some very important issues concerning the railroad was the only thing that impressed them enough to let me pass."

"Let me assure you that today is the last time you will be allowed anywhere near my office."

"That's not very hospitable of you, Corbin."

"I don't intend to be hospitable. My offices are off-limits to anyone other than staff and invited guests."

"Nor are you very polite. Who is the lovely lady you are…uh…entertaining?"

"That's none of your concern."

Jack opened the door and shielded Lena as he escorted her out. He stepped back into the room, but before he closed the door, he called for Brad to join him.

"What are you doing here?" Jack demanded.

"What reason would I have for coming, Corbin? The railroad, of course," Barnaby replied.

Before Jack could respond, Brad entered the room. His shock at seeing Barnaby there was evident.

"Prescott," Barnaby said, greeting the fellow.

"Mr. Barnaby. To what do we owe your visit?"

"My, my," he said with a grin that Jack found irritating. "You are lacking in cordiality, the same as your friend."

"Perhaps that is because I'm as pleased to see you as Jack is."

Jack tired of the insults and wanted nothing more than to get Barnaby out of Lena's office. There was too much here he didn't want the man to see.

"Follow me," he said, moving Barnaby to the door. "My office is down the hall."

"Oh, that's right. This must be the lady's office. You were just visiting."

Jack opened the door, and Brad nearly shoved their intruder from the room.

"Now, why are you here?" Jack said when they reached a spare office he kept on the floor below. An office without a window that overlooked the gaming hall.

"I came to Willowbrook to check on the progress of the railroad, and to make sure you received the list of materials we need."

"Construction on the railroad is progressing as it should, and the workmen have the materials they need to continue working."

"Then why haven't I received any orders to fill for materials, or a check to pay for what our workers need?"

"Probably because we are able to purchase what we need right here in Willowbrook."

"What! Surely you haven't been able to get everything here in Willowbrook."

"We have," Brad said.

"How? I can't believe your merchants are able to purchase

everything you need in Willowbrook."

"They are, and if there's anything we need that they don't have, they purchase it from their suppliers," Jack replied.

"And pay double what it would cost if we purchased it from London manufacturers instead of purchasing it direct."

"No, our suppliers sell everything to us at a reduced price."

"How can they?" Barnaby asked.

"They can because it is worth it to them in the long run. The sooner the railroad is up and running, the sooner profits will increase for every merchant in Willowbrook."

Jack watched Barnaby's expression darken. Instead of being impressed that work on the railroad was progressing at a rapid pace and they were saving money by buying locally, he was angry.

"Is there a problem, Barnaby? Aren't you pleased by the progress the workers are making?"

"Yes, yes. Of course I am."

"Then what is it?"

"N-nothing," Barnaby stammered. "We're simply not used to doing things this way."

"Well, it's how I intend to do things. The citizens of Willowbrook have put their hard-earned money into building this railroad, and they deserve to reap the rewards."

By the look of fury on Barnaby's face and the hostile glare in his eyes, Jack could tell how furious the man was with him.

"Well," he said. "I've found out what I needed to know."

"Will you be in Willowbrook long?" Jack asked.

"No. I have a room at the hotel for the night, then I plan to leave for London in the morning."

"Very well," Jack said. "Have a safe journey back."

Jack and Brad sat in silence while Barnaby left. It wasn't until he was long gone from the club that either of them spoke.

"What do you think he wanted?" Brad asked.

"I'm not sure."

"Neither am I, but did you see how livid he seemed when

you told him that we were buying the supplies we needed locally, and not getting them in London?"

"Yes," Jack said. "It was almost as if he was angry because we weren't going through him to get what we needed."

"Why should he care?"

"I don't know. You'd think he would be glad."

"But he wasn't," Brad said.

"No. He was far from it."

⊱⟫⟩⟩⟨⟨⟨⟪⊰

LENA SAT IN the library and waited for Jack to arrive. They hadn't made plans to meet, but after the way he'd almost pushed her out of her office when Mr. Barnaby showed up, she knew he would come to explain why he'd been so curt with her.

She sat with a glass of wine in her hands and took a sip. Before she could take a second swallow, she heard Franklin open the door and greet Jack. A few seconds later, she heard a soft knock on the library door and watched Jack enter the room.

"I came to apologize," he said from across the room.

"I've been waiting for you."

"I'm sorry, Lena."

"Why didn't you want him to see me? Are you ashamed to be seen with me?"

"No! Heavens no!"

"Then why?"

"Because he is not a good person, and I don't like him. I especially didn't want you to have anything to do with him."

"Who is he, and why did he think he could come up to your office—even though it was my office?" she asked.

"His name is Josiah Barnaby, and he is one of the managing contractors of the railroad."

"Oh. For being so important, you weren't very polite to him."

Jack smiled. "I wasn't, was I?"

"No," Lena said before taking another sip of her wine. "In fact, you were extremely rude."

Jack walked to the sideboard and poured himself a glass of brandy, then carried the crystal decanter back with him and set it on the table. "If you think I was rude when you were there, you should have stayed. I got a lot more impolite."

"I would have stayed," she said, giving him a pointed look. "But you practically threw me out."

"I did, didn't I?" he said with a wink as he sat down beside her.

"Yes, you did. So, what did he want?"

"He wanted to know how we are getting the supplies for the railroad construction. He expected me to go through him for anything Sean Mason—he's our construction foreman—needs."

"But you haven't, have you?"

"No. I get all the supplies I can from merchants in Willow-brook. I go to the hardware store for any tools, nails, and anything else the men need to construct the railroad. I gave our lumber yard a contract for the ties. And a contract to Floyd, the blacksmith, for the iron joints that hold the rails together, and for at least one-third of the iron spikes. It's amazing how much we can provide locally."

"And Mr. Barnaby wasn't happy about that?"

"Not only was he not happy, he was extremely angry. I was completely surprised by his attitude."

"I'm not," Lena said.

"You're not?"

"Absolutely not. He wanted you to send him an itemized payment for the goods you had him purchase in London. He would either deposit the money and keep part of it back, or he would increase the amount he required and keep the overage. Or bill you for premium products when he's buying the lowest quality. Or—"

Lena bit her tongue and watched the full force of Jack's embarrassment sweep across his face. He'd been so preoccupied by his end of the project that he had not given careful scrutiny to what his purchaser was doing. He just expected honorable dealings from the man, as he did all of those involved in the massive project.

"Of course," Jack said. "He could be skimming off the top."

"Is that what you call it?"

"Either skimming or outright stealing. How did you figure that out?"

"I think my mind is just focused on people stealing. It's what people who need money seem to resort to."

"I imagine it does seem like that to someone who would never consider stealing from anyone."

"No, that is something I would never do. I can't think of anything that would make me so desperate for money that I would steal what isn't mine."

"You probably wouldn't. But not everyone is as good and moral as you are."

"You make me sound so virtuous, and I am anything but that."

Jack smiled at her as if he doubted her denial. She loved his smile, and broadened her own. Which was a mistake. She saw his eyes suddenly warm, and worked to quell her own eager response. She had to distract them both. And quickly.

"I've been wanting to ask you something," she said, sitting back on the sofa. "Something that has nothing to do with the railroad."

Jack relaxed beside her, sitting so close that the warmth from his body traveled through her clothing to heat her flesh. It wasn't helping. Not a bit.

"What would you like to know?"

"Actually, it's a question about Brad."

"Ah…" he said. "You want to know more about how he got the horrific scars he can't hide."

"Essie is the one who wants to know. Because she can't see, it helps her if she can outline a person's face with her fingers. That way she can tell what they look like."

"And she tried to touch Brad's face, but he wouldn't let her."

"Yes. So she asked me what he looked like, and I described him as best as I could, but I didn't do him justice."

"What did you tell her he looked like?" Jack asked.

"I said he had some horrific scars on his face that started at his temple and ran to below his jaw. As if someone had peeled the skin from his face."

"That's a pretty fair description. What did she say when you told her?"

"She wanted to know more about what happened. I said I didn't really know any more, but I would ask you."

Jack stared at the liquor in his glass, then breathed a heavy sigh. "What happened to him was my fault."

"*Your* fault?"

"Yes. As I told you, during the war, I was sent on assignment to infiltrate the Russian camp and get certain information—vital information concerning the enemy's next battle strategy. I was sent because my commanders didn't want the Russians to know we saw their battle plans if maps went missing. So, I was sent to memorize the maps without the Russians knowing we had seen them. Brad volunteered to come with me to watch my back."

"And they sent you because of your ability to remember everything perfectly just by seeing it once."

"Exactly. The same way I can remember the cards that have been played. I can read something once and recall it exactly as written."

Lena looked at him with admiration. "That's an amazing gift, Jack."

"It's unusual, I'll grant you that, but I'm not sure whether I consider it a gift, or a curse."

"I consider it a gift," Lena said. "A rare gift. But go on."

"Things didn't go as planned. Brad and I made it into the Russian camp and found the papers. I read them, then put them back where they were, but as we were leaving, we were caught.

"The enemy officers interrogated me. They wanted to know what I'd seen, as well as a list of details about what our plans were for our next confrontation. They wanted to know how many soldiers were in our platoon, and when we were going to attack. Of course, I didn't tell them anything."

"So they tortured you," Lena said in a soft, husky voice.

"The officer who interrogated me had a whip, and he enjoyed using it," Jack said through gritted teeth.

Lena reached over and held his hand.

"I vowed I wouldn't reveal anything, no matter what they did to me. As if they realized I wasn't going to tell them anything, they gave up torturing me and tortured Brad instead. Day after day they beat him, even though I told them Brad didn't know anything."

"But they didn't believe you, did they?" Lena said, fighting the tears that filled her eyes.

"Oh, they believed me. They *knew* Brad didn't know anything, and they told me that any time I wanted them to stop, all I had to do was tell them what they wanted to know.

"Every time they brought Brad back and threw him into the cell with me, his body was so bruised and bloody I hardly recognized him. Then they stopped beating him and started to skin him alive."

Lena couldn't comprehend how anyone could do something so horrific to another human being. The tears she'd struggled to keep from falling ran down her cheeks.

Jack paused to fill his glass with more brandy. He took a long swallow, then held the glass in his hands and stared at the floor. "Dear God, I couldn't bear his screams when they ripped the flesh from his body. Finally, I couldn't take it any longer. I told him to pretend he was dead and I'd take out as many of the enemy as I could."

"Did you?"

"Yes. It was a brutal struggle, which I nearly lost. But by some miracle, my commanding officer arrived to rescue us, though not until I'd been shot and stabbed several times. That was the closest I've ever come to dying. When Brad and I healed, I knew if I intended to realize my dream of opening my gentlemen's club, I needed to get on with it."

"That's why you made Brad your partner, isn't it? You felt you needed to repay him for what he went through in your place."

"No, I made him my partner because he's the best friend anyone could ever have. And I love him like a brother."

"You are very lucky to have a friend like Brad, and he's lucky to have you."

"Like I'm lucky to have a friend like you," he said, wrapping his arm around her and pulling her close.

Lena had not been prepared for the ambush and could summon no defenses. There was nothing for her to do but surrender.

CHAPTER TEN

JACK WAS DESPERATE to hold Lena, desperate to have her close to him. Desperate to kiss her.

He didn't know how it happened, but somehow over the last month she'd become very special to him. She was the woman he thought he'd never find. Someone he could talk to, who understood what he'd survived. Someone with whom he could share the horrors that had happened to him—who could help him heal, help him dispel the memory of events that caused nightmares to terrorize his sleep.

He lowered his head and pressed his lips to hers. She eagerly returned his kiss and wrapped her arms around his neck. She held on to him as if she wanted to never let him go. And he answered her passion with the desire he felt for her.

This was what he'd dreamed of experiencing with a woman, a need and desire that surpassed anything he'd ever felt before. She was everything he wanted and needed, and for the first time in his life, he imagined what life could be with a woman like Lena always at his side.

He kissed her again, then held her close to him. His heart thundered in his chest, and his breathing rushed out with the same desperation as Lena's.

He sat back, feeling well sated and recognizing the satisfaction that bloomed in *her* eyes, as well. He leaned toward her and kissed her on the forehead.

"So, what are you going to tell your sister about Brad?"

Lena dropped her head on Jack's shoulder and breathed a heavy sigh. "I'm tempted to tell her everything you told me, but I'm more inclined to make her wait to hear the story from Brad himself. She shouldn't know what happened to him until he trusts her enough to tell her himself."

Jack gazed into her eyes and smiled. "You need to be careful, Lena. You're so close to being perfect that I'm starting to fall in love with you."

"Would that be so terrible, Jack?"

"No, that would only be terrible if it was impossible for you to love me in return."

"Then you have nothing to worry about," she replied, and Jack couldn't stop himself from taking her in his arms and kissing her again. Then again.

And again.

THE NEXT FEW weeks went by so rapidly, Lena had a difficult time finishing one day's work before it was time to go to work again. To make things more stressful, the club was busier than ever. Jack said he didn't remember it ever being this busy. But everyone was coming to the popular meeting place to hear the latest news concerning the railroad.

Jack and Brad had become very comfortable with their shared schedule. Jack spent the greater part of every day taking care of business for the railroad and working the club's daytime hours, while Brad worked evenings and through the night. This left Brad free every afternoon, and one could almost always find him at Corbin House with Essie.

On nice days, the two went for walks in the garden, then sat in the gazebo or on one of the benches that lined the paths, and

Brad would describe the flowers that were blooming and the riot of colors that made the garden come alive.

Other days, when it rained or the weather was too chilly to sit outside, they spent the afternoons indoors. Essie and Brad were going through Jack's extensive library with amazing speed. Lena told herself that she was going to have to visit the Page Turner Bookshop and purchase several new books so they didn't run out of novels to read. The thought of it brought a warm glow to her chest. With her new salary, she was able to go well beyond personal expenditures. Buying books for Essie was something she never could have managed before Jack had come into their lives. Now she could afford the occasional frill, and it was a liberating feeling that she savored.

Lena smiled when she thought of how perfectly Essie and Brad got along. Most days when she returned home from work, she could hear them talking and laughing. Essie had never been so happy, and Lena knew that being with Brad was what caused that happiness.

Today when Lena went down to breakfast, she was surprised to see Essie already there.

"My, you are up early this morning," she said, putting strips of bacon and coddled eggs on her plate. "What's the occasion?"

"Rupert told me yesterday that if the weather was good and I rose early, we could go for a ride. Well, the weather is good, so I got out of bed, dressed, and came down to eat a little something so I'm ready when he arrives."

"You enjoy riding, don't you, Essie?"

"Oh, Lena. I do, ever so much. I didn't know there was such freedom in riding, even if Rupert won't let me go too fast yet."

Lena smiled. "Well, I'm glad to hear that. You haven't been riding all that long, so you shouldn't go too fast yet."

"Have you ever ridden?"

"Once or twice," Lena answered. "Father took me out a few times and let me ride the horse at the vicarage."

Essie laughed. "That wasn't really riding. Our horse at the

vicarage was so old he could barely move, let alone work up to a gallop."

"I have to admit you're right. He couldn't go very fast at all."

Lena finished her breakfast and rose.

"Would you walk me to the stable, Lena? There's no sense in making Rupert walk to the house when I could be there when he's ready."

"Of course I can. Are you ready to go?"

"Yes. I'm ready."

Lena looped her arm through Essie's, and together they walked to the stable. When she had Essie safely delivered, she returned to the waiting carriage and went to work. She couldn't believe how perfect her life was. Just when she'd feared she and Essie would be forced to live on the street, Jack had appeared and changed their lives. She owed him so much. As much as she'd grown to love him.

When the carriage stopped at the back of the club, Lena alighted and entered the building as she did every day.

"You look cheery this morning," Jack greeted her when she reached her room. She met him in the hallway with a cup of coffee in his hands.

"I am. Essie was up when I left. Rupert is taking her for a riding lesson, and she was as excited as if it were Christmas morning."

Jack smiled as he followed her into her office.

"It's wonderful to see Essie so happy. I owe you so much, Jack. More than I can ever repay you."

"You don't have to repay me for anything. You're helping me as much as I helped you."

Lena smiled, knowing that wasn't quite true. But it made her happy to know Jack thought she contributed something.

"I have some news that might spoil your mood, however," he added.

"What?"

"I got word this morning that Josiah Barnaby and Wilson

Hanover will arrive sometime this morning."

"Was Mr. Barnaby the man you didn't want me to meet the last time he was here?"

"Yes. And I hope you don't have to see him today, either."

"Who is Wilson Hanover?" she asked.

"He's the president of the railroad investors. From London."

"Oh my," Lena said. "I'll be sure to stay in my office and keep the door locked."

"That would be wise. Hopefully, they'll only be here a couple of hours, then return to London today."

"Do you know why they're coming?"

"I have an idea. I think they're upset because I pay the bills through the Willowbrook office instead of the London office. They don't get to handle any of the money that way."

"I told you why I think they don't like that."

"Yes, and I think you are correct. But I hope the reason is that they simply don't trust me enough. That would put a better light on everything than thinking that Barnaby is stealing from the railroad account."

"Speaking of stealing," Lena ventured, "have you decided what you're going to do with our suspected thief at table one?"

Jack finished the coffee in his cup, then stepped over to the spy portal to look down on the floor. "His name is Russell Walters, and he's the oldest of eight children. His father died last year in a farming accident, and he works as many hours as he can to earn as much as he can. He sends almost all of his money home to provide for his mother and his brothers and sisters."

"Oh, Jack," Lena said in a choked voice.

"He isn't here yet," Jack said, "but I made up my mind to speak with him when he comes in."

"What are you going to do?"

"I'm not sure. I'll decide after I've talked to him."

Lena wanted to ask Jack not to do anything to the young man, but this wasn't her business, and she didn't have the right to tell Jack what to do.

"You don't have an opinion, Lena?"

"No," she replied. "I'll leave this decision to you."

Jack leaned close to her and kissed her on the cheek, then turned to leave. "I've got a lot to do before our guests arrive, so I'd best get busy. Lock the door after me."

Jack left the room, and Lena started on her accounts. She entered the money amount from each table into the ledger, then sat up and stretched her stiff muscles before she made out her bank deposit. She took a turn around the office, then paused to focus on the floor below. It was moderately busy, and she watched the floor manager move to table one to speak with Russell Walters. Lena saw him motion to the floor above, then Russell climbed the stairs and walked to Jack's office.

Lena knew what that meant. Jack had sent for Russell, and there was a possibility that when he exited Jack's office he would no longer have a position in the club, or perhaps he would be held until the authorities took him away.

She closed her eyes and said a silent prayer that God would be with Jack, and Russell Walters.

⟫⟫⟫⟪⟪⟪

JACK SAT IN the chair behind his desk and waited for Walters to come to see him.

"Do you know how you're going to handle this?" Brad asked, waiting at the door to let Walters in when he knocked.

"I'll do what I have to do," Jack answered. "I can't afford to have a thief work for me. That's one of the agreements I made with Lord Murdock. I told him that I would run an honest establishment, and I intend to do just that."

"I simply can't believe Walters thought he could get away with stealing from us. But if it not for Lena, I'm betting we still wouldn't suspect him."

Jack slowly nodded. "You're right. This railroad project has caused me to lose track of what's going on in my club."

"And I wasn't any help to you, either."

"That's because you were trying to do my job as well as your own."

"That's not an excuse, but it's something we're going to have to consider when the railroad project is finished."

Jack grunted his agreement and didn't continue their conversation when there was a knock on the door. Brad reached for the handle and opened it.

"Come in, Russell," Jack said. "Have a seat."

"Thank you, Mr. Corbin, but I prefer to stand."

"Very well. Do you know why you're here?"

Jack studied the young man standing in front of him and noticed the calm composure. At first, Walters's stoic self-control angered him, but there was something about his humble self-discipline that Jack admired.

"Yes, Mr. Corbin. I'm sure I know why I'm here. You undoubtedly discovered that I have been stealing from you."

"You admit that you've been stealing?"

Walters lowered his gaze to the floor. "Yes," he said in a hushed tone.

"Why?" Jack said, unable to hide his anger. "Don't you think you're paid enough for the work you do?"

"Oh, no! You are more than generous, Mr. Corbin."

"Then why? Why did you resort to stealing from me?"

For the first time, the young man looked as if he might break down.

"*Why?*"

"I had to. I had no choice."

"Why didn't you have a choice?"

"Because my family is in danger of losing our farm, and if we do, my family will starve."

Jack was stunned. He turned to Brad and saw the same look of shock on his partner's face.

"Explain why your family will starve," Jack said, pouring a

half glass of brandy into a glass and handing it to Walters.

The young man took a gulp, then sat in the chair Jack had offered him earlier. "My father died in an accident on our farm a couple of months ago. I have my mum and seven brothers and sisters to take care of. I'm the oldest and the only one who earns a living. My next two brothers work the farm and love farming, but when Pa died, our landlord refused to let them prove they could manage as good as Pa. He demanded the full year's rent or he was going to kick them off the land."

Walters reached into his pocket, brought out a piece of paper, and handed it to Jack.

"Here is an accounting of all the money I've taken from you so far."

Jack looked at it, then handed it to Brad.

"I intend to pay it all back from my wages. I was just going to take enough so the boys could pay the rent so they'd be safe until next winter, so Mum and the girls would have a home to live in. By then, the boys will have the money from the sale of the crops and the livestock to afford the next year's rent."

"Do you have enough money to pay the rent so your family won't lose their home?" Jack asked.

"Almost. I only need about twelve quid more."

"Mr. Prescott. Get one hundred pounds from upstairs and give it to Mr. Walters."

"Yes, Jack," Brad said, and left the room.

"That's too much, Mr. Corbin. I only need twelve," Walters protested.

"Give the leftover amount to your mum to make sure she has enough food and sundries to last the winter."

"Oh, thank you, Mr. Corbin. I…I don't know what to say."

"You are welcome, Walters. Next time, though, come to me first. Don't resort to stealing."

"Oh, there won't be a next time, sir. My brothers will do a great job running the farm. Pa was a good teacher, and he taught them everything they need to know."

"But you didn't want to farm?" Jack asked.

"No. I wanted to do something different, and when I got the job here, I realized this was it. Maybe someday I might even be lucky enough to own my own gentlemen's club."

"Yes," Jack said with a smile. "Maybe you will."

"But if I don't," Walters said, "I'll be happy enough working here. *If* I still have a job."

"Yes, you still have a job. But next time you need something, you come to me first."

"I will, sir. And thank you."

Jack watched the young man leave, his posture a bit finer than it had been when he entered. It felt good knowing he'd dealt fairly with Walters. He could easily have dealt briskly and harshly, under the circumstances. But Walters seemed the sort who would not only keep his word, he would be a long-term asset to the club.

So far, today was turning out rather satisfactorily.

CHAPTER ELEVEN

JACK STAYED IN his second-floor office and worked on the railroad books. He knew Barnaby and Hanover would arrive soon, and he didn't want them to find him in his third-floor office. Mostly, he didn't want Barnaby anywhere near Lena or his accounting ledgers.

Before long, Brad entered the room. "Your guests are here. Do you want me to bring them up?"

"No, I'll go down to meet them," Jack answered with a sigh of indecision that bordered on frustration. "Did you get Russell taken care of?"

"Yes. You handled that nicely, Jack."

"I was impressed with the young man. He has a lot of character. He would have made a great soldier."

"I'm glad the war is over and he didn't have to serve. I often think how different my life would have been if I hadn't served."

"But if you hadn't served, we wouldn't have met, or gone into partnership. And if we hadn't started this club, we wouldn't have had to hire Lena, and you wouldn't have met Essie, and…"

"All right. All right. You made your point," Brad said, laughing. "And we wouldn't be filthy rich, either."

"No, we wouldn't. Now, aren't you glad you joined Her Majesty's army?"

"When you put it that way, I guess I am. Now, are you sure

you don't want me to bring your guests up?"

"No, I'll go down. I have to take them to the railroad site and let them speak to Sean Mason."

"I'm sure he's as anxious to speak with them as you are," Brad said.

"I don't doubt it. Every time they meet with him, they have a dozen questions and complaints."

"I know. But it's good that Hanover is with Barnaby today. At least he has a brain in that head of his. I think Barnaby was absent when God handed out gray matter."

Jack couldn't help but laugh at Brad's comment. "When we're gone, take the deposit to the bank. Take George with you, but don't go until we're gone."

"You don't want our guests to see how much money we take in?" Brad asked.

"No, the less they know about our business, the better off we'll be. Now, let's get this pleasant afternoon over with," Jack said before walking to the door and going down a flight of stairs to meet with Hanover and Barnaby.

Jack found the railroad managers roaming the floor, stopping to watch the card games in progress.

"Hello, Corbin," Hanover said in greeting. "You have quite the fine establishment here."

"Thank you," Jack said, watching the rapt attention Barnaby paid to the cards being played and the bets placed. He was obviously someone who was more than mildly familiar with games of chance.

"Are you ready to go?" Hanover asked when Barnaby seemed reluctant to leave the gaming tables.

"Yes," Barnaby answered absently, but Jack was sure he would have stayed behind if given the chance.

Jack led the way out of the card room and through the front room, where a sizable group of men had gathered to discuss the latest progress on the railroad.

"So, what is the consensus of the railroad coming through

Willowbrook?" Hanover asked when they were in Jack's carriage and on their way to the construction site.

"The majority of residents can't wait for the railroad to be up and running," Jack said. "When we return to Willowbrook, we'll stop by the train depot. The builders have made remarkable progress on it."

"I'm impressed by how quickly you're getting the railroad built, Corbin," Hanover said. "I've been involved with several such projects, and none of them have been built so rapidly. What are you doing that's different?"

"We're providing as much of the materials as we can right here in Willowbrook. The project managers turn in a list of items they'll need on a daily basis, and Sean orders them locally. Some items, of course, have to be ordered from London, but we can order those far enough in advance that they arrive before they're needed. Because of that, there is little if any downtime on the actual construction. Everything has progressed swiftly so far."

"Did you hear that, Barnaby?" Hanover said, turning to face his partner. "Make a note of how Corbin runs the Willowbrook project. We'll implement his procedure on all future railroad projects. That should cut costs down by at least a third."

"Yes," Barnaby replied, but Jack noticed his expression, which indicated that he was anything but pleased.

"No wonder your club is so successful," Hanover continued. "You have a talent for superb management."

Hanover's words of praise weren't endearing him to Barnaby. In fact, they seemed to alienate the man.

"We must be at the site," Jack said as the carriage slowed.

When the carriage stopped, Jack alighted first, followed by Hanover, then Barnaby. Sean Mason saw them and came to join them.

After introductions were made, Sean gave them a tour of the site. To say Hanover was impressed was an understatement. He profusely complimented Jack and Sean. This only seemed to anger Barnaby more, and Jack couldn't help but wonder why.

Surely his position with Hanover wasn't that insecure.

But maybe it was.

JACK COULD THINK of little else all the way back to the club than the way Barnaby had reacted to everything Hanover said, and how unimpressed he seemed to be when Hanover complimented Jack. There was something about Barnaby's anger that bothered Jack. It was unnatural.

When they reached the club, Hanover requested a private meeting. Jack had an idea why he wanted to meet, but he was reluctant to hear any proposal Hanover might make. He could hardly refuse to at least hear him out, but that wouldn't change the decision Jack would give him.

Barnaby left to visit the gaming room, and Jack led Hanover to a private room where they could talk without being overheard.

"I'll get right to the point," Hanover said when Jack handed him a glass of brandy and they were seated. "As you probably know, I am more than a little impressed with you. You exhibit several of the traits I look for in the managing partners of my organization."

"Thank you, Mr. Hanover, but if you are going to offer me a position with your organization, I will save us both a great deal of time. I have worked my whole life to start Jackson's Gentlemen's Club and make it a success, and I have no intention of leaving it now. Or ever."

"Except you haven't heard me out. I am not asking you to come work for me. I am offering you a partnership—part ownership."

Jack was taken aback by Hanover's offer. "That's more than generous, Mr. Hanover, but the answer is the same. I have no desire to give up what I have here."

"Do you have any idea the amount of money I'm talking

about?"

"No, nor do I care."

"Please, hear me out."

Jack heard Hanover's offer but didn't need to consider it. He had more interest in the questions he wanted answered about Barnaby.

"How long has Barnaby been with you?" Jack asked after taking a sip of his brandy.

"Going on ten years, if I remember correctly."

"Why haven't you offered him what you offered me?"

Hanover smiled, then chuckled. "How do you know I haven't?"

"Because if you had, he would be your partner now. He likes money too much to refuse your offer."

Hanover sat back in his chair with a serious expression on his face. "Yes, he does," he replied. "He also enjoys gambling too much, but he doesn't have any skill at it."

"In other words, he loses more than he wins," Jack said.

"Not only does he lose more than he wins, but he loses more than he can afford to."

"Are you saying he has a gambling *problem?*"

"Yes, that's what I'm saying."

"I see," Jack said, thinking he should cut this conversation short and go to the floor to stop Barnaby from running up too big a gambling loss.

"Don't worry, Corbin. I'll cover his debt before we leave. I won't let him leave you with a debt you can't collect."

"That's very generous of you, but may I ask you a personal question?"

"Of course."

"If you know Barnaby has a gambling problem, why do you keep him on?"

"I ask myself that same question all the time, and the answer is that I woefully lack the courage to fire him. Josiah Barnaby is my nephew, you see. My youngest sister's son. And years ago I promised her that I would take him under my wing and break him of his compulsion to gamble."

Hanover finished the brandy in his glass but refused Jack's offer for more.

"Obviously I have failed so far. Instead of curbing his gambling, Josiah has run up debts all over London that he cannot pay."

"I assume that you realize how dangerous that can be," Jack said, knowing he was stating something that was none of his business.

"Yes, so this time when he came to me for more money, I refused him. Hopefully, that will teach him."

Jack doubted Barnaby would curb his gambling. He'd seen too many gamblers who swore they could quit gambling anytime they wanted to but weren't able to. Too many who thought if they just kept gambling, they would win enough to get themselves out of debt. But they never did, and eventually the men they owed money came after them.

He hoped Barnaby was one of the lucky ones, but he doubted it.

"Are you sure I can't talk you into joining me?" Hanover said when he'd finished his brandy and was preparing to leave.

"I'm sure, sir. I appreciate your offer, but I enjoy it here in Willowbrook, and this is where I want to stay."

"If you ever change your mind, Jack, let me know. The offer is always open."

"Thank you, Mr. Hanover. I appreciate your offer."

Jack opened the door for Hanover, and they left the private room together. They walked to the game room and looked around but didn't see Barnaby at any of the tables.

"Do you see him?" Hanover asked.

"No—perhaps he wanted to show you that your threat worked. Perhaps he wanted to prove to you he could walk out of a gaming hall without stopping to gamble."

"I hope you're right. I can't think of anything that would

make me happier."

Just then, Barnaby entered the hall slightly out of breath and a little disheveled.

"Where were you, Josiah?" Hanover asked. "You look like you've just run a race."

"Not a race," Barnaby said. "I went for a walk. I knew if I stayed here, I'd sit down at one of the tables and lose some money. I'm taking your advice, Uncle, and curbing my gaming."

"Good for you, lad. You'll make me and your mother so happy."

"I knew it was what you wanted. I'm trying, you see."

"You made me a happy man. Now, are you ready to head back to London?"

"Yes," Barnaby said.

Jack walked them out to their carriage and waited until they took the road back to London. He hadn't believed one word of Barnaby's tale about curbing his gambling. Nor that he'd gone for a walk. He was out of breath because he'd been running.

"Did you know the gentleman who just left in that carriage, Mr. Corbin?" George, his carriage driver, asked.

"Yes, George. Why?"

"I just returned from taking Miss Osbourne home, and that young man watched the lady get into the carriage, then followed us all the way to Corbin House at a run."

"Bloody hell," Jack muttered.

CHAPTER TWELVE

BRAD WALKED THE short distance to Corbin House and knocked on the door. Franklin opened it to him before he finished knocking.

"Is Miss Esther here?" he asked, knowing that she would be. Where else would she be?

"I'm sorry Mr. Prescott, but Miss Esther is out riding."

"Oh," Brad said, unable to conceal his disappointment. "Is Rupert with her?"

"Yes, Mr. Prescott, but they should be back soon. They've been gone quite some time already."

"I think I'll wait for them," he said. "I walked here, so I don't have my horse or carriage with me."

"That is perfectly fine. Would you like to wait inside?"

"No, I think I'll wait for Miss Esther outside."

"Very good, sir." Franklin started to close the door then stopped. "I see them approaching now, sir."

"So do I," Brad said, and started off for the stable. He reached Esther just in time to assist her from her horse. "She's turning into quite the rider, isn't she, Rupert?"

"That she is, Mr. Prescott," Rupert answered.

"That's because I have such excellent teachers," Essie said, looping her arm through Brad's elbow and walking with him back to the house. "Can we sit in the garden?" she asked when they reached the library.

"Of course," Brad said, and led her to the French doors that opened onto the terrace.

"It's a beautiful day, isn't it?" Essie said.

Brad smiled. "Yes, beautiful. The sun is shining, and there is just a gentle breeze."

"I think that's what I most wish I could see. The colors of the sky and the clouds and the grass and the leaves on the trees. Lena tries to describe them to me, but I truly wish I could see them just once. She makes them sound so beautiful."

"They are, Essie. The colors of nature are the most beautiful sights in the world."

Essie breathed a deep sigh, and Brad heard so much regret in the sound that he had to fight an ache in his chest. He couldn't stop himself from holding her. The feel of her in his arms was the most exhilarating sensation he'd ever experienced.

"And I would like to see your face," she said, nestling her cheek against his chest.

Brad chuckled. "I'm glad you can't, Essie. One look at my face and you would run away in fright."

"I wouldn't. Being blind has given me the opportunity to judge people by their goodness inside, not their features on the outside. And you, Brad, possess a remarkable amount of kindness and virtue on the inside."

Essie's words warmed his heart. It had been so long since he'd had anyone see him for who he was inside and not his deformities.

Suddenly, Brad realized he cared more for Essie than he thought he could care for anyone ever again. Without considering what he was doing, he wrapped his arms more tightly around her.

Essie skimmed her hands up his chest and wound her arms around his neck. He knew she must have felt the scars that marred his chest, but she didn't react as if she'd noticed. She held him tightly and met his lips when he kissed her as if she'd been anticipating this and was hungry for it.

His kiss was deep and all-consuming. He couldn't believe how desperate he was to show her the passion he had stored inside him, the intense passion that burned inside him and ached to be released.

She met his kiss with a hunger that matched his. It was as if she'd stored an equally uncontrollable amount of desire that was as eager to find release—easily as intense as the passion that was trapped inside him.

Brad kissed her again and again, each mating of their lips assuaging a need that was desperate to find completion.

After several tumultuous minutes, Brad ended their kiss. Only then was he able to consider the ramifications of what had just happened. Their kisses had weakened Essie's knees. Her breaths were coming in rapid gasps, the same as his. She was pressed close to him and had her head nestled against his chest. Her hands cradled his cheeks, touching the horrific scars that marred his features.

He tried to turn his head to avoid her touch, but she would not let him.

"No, Brad. Don't turn away from me. Let me know you."

He froze, desperate to escape her touch, yet unable to.

She ran her fingers over his high cheekbones then down the length of his face. She followed the scar that altered his face, making him appear a grotesque figure that women had a difficult time looking at. She traced the lines of his jaw, stopping at the cleft in his chin, a cleft that every Prescott male had, then skimmed her fingers up the opposite side of his face and across his high forehead.

"You have such strong features," she said, cupping her palm to his cheek again. "You are a very handsome man, Brad. Don't ever think you aren't."

"And you are a very beautiful woman, Essie. One of the most beautiful I've ever met."

She smiled. "I didn't know you had such a golden tongue,

sir."

Brad laughed. It felt strange to laugh at her silly comment. It had been a long time since he'd had something to laugh about. A long time since he'd had something that had caused him to smile. And he owed his newfound laughter and smile to Essie.

"I think we had better continue our walk, sir, or I'm going to embarrass myself and ask you to kiss me again."

"I take it you enjoyed it," he teased.

"Of course I did. Didn't you?"

Brad wanted to laugh again but thought she might misinterpret it to mean he didn't take her question seriously. He turned her in his arms and faced her as if she could see his sincere expression. "Miss Osbourne, I want you to know that I've never enjoyed a kiss more than the one we shared. Our kiss was perfect."

"Thank you, Brad," she whispered.

"You are welcome, Essie." He took a deep breath and released it slowly. "Now, I think we need to continue our walk before I embarrass myself and kiss you again. And again."

Essie looped her arm through his, and they moved forward. "This has been a perfect day. Probably the most perfect day ever," she said, and tightened her hold on his arm.

Brad thought he might have died and gone to heaven.

Jack strode to Brad's office, not really expecting him to be there but wanting to tell him that Barnaby was Hanover's nephew. And he had a gambling problem. Jack had seen enough club members with gambling problems to know what a life-destroying habit it was. He also knew how difficult, if not impossible, it was to overcome that compulsion.

He knocked, then entered the office, but found it empty. There was only one place he thought Brad might be—the same place he was every afternoon at this time.

Jack locked the doors to every room he'd opened and left the club. He took his horse and rode the short distance to Corbin House. Lena would be there, as well as Brad and Essie. It would be best if he told Lena and Brad what he'd discovered about Barnaby. She needed to be warned.

He dismounted and walked to the front door. Franklin opened the door before he reached it.

"Is Miss Lena here, Franklin?"

"Yes, Mr. Corbin. She's in the library. Mr. Prescott and Miss Esther are in the garden."

"Thank you, Franklin," he said, and went to the library. The door was open, and he entered without knocking.

"Jack," Lena greeted him. "Is something wrong?"

"No, Lena. I just wanted to speak with Brad, and when I couldn't find him at the club, I knew he'd be here."

She smiled. "Yes, he and Essie are in the garden. I didn't want to disturb them, so I came in here to wait until they come back into the house."

"I think they've formed quite a friendship," Jack said, pouring himself a glass of brandy.

"I think it's more than friendship, Jack. Have you seen the way they look at each other?"

"Yes," Jack said before lifting his glass to his mouth and taking a sip. "What do you think of that?"

Lena closed the book she'd been reading and placed it beside her on the settee. "I don't know, Jack. A part of me is happy for them. I've always wanted Essie to find love, and now I think she has."

"But...?"

"But..." Lena swallowed past the lump in her throat. "Essie's blind, Jack. How can she be someone's wife?"

Jack reached for Lena's hands and squeezed her fingers.

"She will have to have constant help," she continued. "What if they have children?"

"Are you worried that Brad won't be able to take care of Essie? Are you afraid she will be neglected?"

"No," she answered firmly. "But she will be a huge expense."

Jack couldn't contain his laughter.

"What?" Lena said.

"You talk about the cost of caring for Essie as if Brad can't afford to take care of her. Do you have any idea how wealthy he is? Do you have any idea how wealthy *I* am?"

"I know the club makes a lot of money," she answered. "I do the books, you know."

"Then you should have a fair idea of what our daily intake is."

"Yes, but you have a huge amount of expenses, too."

"Money is something neither Brad nor I will ever have to worry about. Even after I pay all the expenses for the club and Corbin House, there is still enough money remaining that I can give Brad his share and have a goodly amount left over. I have enough money in the bank that even if I never added another pound to it, I'd still have more than enough to live lavishly for the rest of my life. No, Lena. Money is one thing you will never have to be concerned over."

Jack was relieved when the French doors opened and Brad and Essie entered the library.

"Jack and Lena are here, Essie," Brad said, showing her to the sofa nearest where Jack and Lena sat. It already seemed so natural for him to describe their surroundings to Essie, to let her know who they would be joining, to fill in the puzzle pieces her mind was busily assembling.

"Were you out enjoying the nice weather?" Lena asked.

"Yes," Essie answered. "It is a beautiful day. Have you been home long?"

"Not long," Lena replied.

"Good. Would you like some tea?" Essie asked.

"Yes, I would. Let me ring for it."

But Essie was already up and moving easily toward the bell-pull. She returned to her place beside Brad without the slightest hesitation.

He stood to help her sit, then walked to the sideboard and poured himself a brandy, then brought the decanter over and filled Jack's snifter.

"I take it you have something you need to discuss with me," Brad said when he settled himself on the sofa next to Essie.

"I do," Jack said. "I discovered some interesting facts today concerning our two guests, Hanover and Barnaby."

"I take it that you are concerned by what you learned," Brad said.

"Let's say our guests bear watching." Jack set his glass on the table in front of him. "At least, Barnaby does. I discovered that he is not a partner or an investor. Josiah Barnaby is Wilson Hanover's nephew."

"Well," Brad said. "That *is* interesting."

"Yes. Hanover told me that his sister asked him to take Barnaby under his wing to straighten him out."

"Straighten him out from what?" Brad asked.

"It seems Barnaby has a severe gambling problem."

"That explains why he was so upset when you decided to purchase whatever you could here in Willowbrook rather than having him purchase them in London."

"Why would that upset him?" Essie asked.

"While going through several of the orders from previous projects, I discovered that Barnaby inflated the amounts of items he said he ordered," Jack said.

"So, the amount that was paid for wood for the ties and metal for the rails was an amount higher than what the company owed," Brad explained.

"Which allowed Barnaby to pocket the excess money," Lena finished.

"Which lost the company several thousand pounds, and covered Barnaby's gambling debts," Jack added.

"Except, now that *you* pay for the materials for the railroad, he can't steal from his uncle's company any longer," Brad added.

"Which makes him unable to pay his gambling debts, no doubt making a large number of clubs and money lenders very angry."

"Does he owe your club much money?" Lena asked.

"No. And even if he did, his uncle guaranteed he would cover the debts. He doesn't want the club stuck with his nephew's vowels."

Brad focused his attention on Jack. "What do you think he's going to do, Jack?"

"I expect him to return without his uncle. He's no doubt run out of places that will extend him credit in London and needs to find other places where he can win back his losses."

"Which he will never do," Lena said.

"No," Jack replied. "Which he will never do."

"Well," Brad said. "Since he isn't a member, we can refuse to allow him to gamble until he fills out the necessary papers, which will take months."

Jack smiled. "Now I need to get back to the club. I didn't get as much done as I wanted today."

"I'll go with you. I want to make sure the doormen know not to admit Barnaby, even though he was a guest earlier today."

Jack and Brad bade Lena and Essie goodbye, and left.

"There's something else, isn't there, Jack?" Brad said when they were on their way.

Jack laughed. "You know me too well, my friend. It's almost frightening."

"Yes, I almost know you better than you know yourself. So, what is it?"

"George told me that Barnaby saw Lena leave the club today and followed her carriage to find out where she was going. Now he knows where she lives."

"Bloody hell," Brad spat.

"My feelings exactly."

"What do you think he'll do?"

"I don't know, but it won't be good."

CHAPTER THIRTEEN

S OMETHING WAS WRONG. Lena felt it clear to her toes.
It had been nearly a week since Jack related what Hanover had told him about his nephew, and since that day, Lena had
noticed extra security at the doors of the club, as well as more
floor supervisors than usual.

Several times she'd attempted to ask Jack why there were
more guards, but he refused to give her an answer.

But what bothered her the most was that George was no
longer alone when he collected her in the morning or when he
drove her home when she was done—there was always another
guard riding with him.

This told Lena that Jack wasn't only concerned that Barnaby
would run up a huge debt, but that he posed a threat to the club.
Surely Jack didn't think that he would try to rob him.

Lena was done for the day and left by her customary route,
stepping into the carriage when she reached the alley yard.
George closed the door behind her, and the carriage tilted when
he climbed atop.

She would be glad when she reached home. For some reason,
she was quite exhausted today. Yesterday's receipts were larger
than usual, and she'd had to re-count the money that went to the
bank several times to make sure it was correct. Jack had said that
he expected receipts to increase even more when the railroad was

completed. He told her he expected more people to travel to Willowbrook to do business, then stay overnight and return to London the next morning. His thinking was that they'd need someplace to relax, eat a good meal, and pass the time by playing a few hands of cards. What better place to do all three than Jackson's Gentlemen's Club?

Lena made a note that she'd have to arrive at the club earlier in the mornings to complete her work, if that were the case. Or perhaps even ask for an assistant.

The carriage traveled the distance from the club to Corbin House, and she arrived home in record time. "Thank you, George. I'll see you in the morning."

"Yes, Miss Osbourne. Have a nice evening."

"I will," she replied as she went to the door.

Franklin waited, as usual, with the door open.

"Good evening, Miss Osbourne. How was your day?"

"Busy, Franklin. It was quite busy. Is my sister in the library?"

"No, miss. She and Rupert are out riding. She should be back soon, though. They've been gone quite a while already."

"Then I'll wait for her in the library."

"Yes, miss. I'll tell her when she returns."

"Thank you, Franklin," Lena said, then went to the library to sit for a while. She opened the book she'd been reading, but before she finished the first page, her eyes closed and she fell asleep.

"EXCUSE ME, MISS Magdalena?"

A voice echoed in her head.

"Miss Magdalena?"

It took Lena several moments to realize someone was calling her. She opened her eyes and saw their butler standing over her.

"I'm sorry, Franklin. I must have fallen asleep."

"Yes, miss. But I thought you should know Miss Esther hasn't returned yet, and it's getting quite late."

Lena was startled awake. Her heart thundered in her breast, and she couldn't breathe.

Just then, the stable master appeared outside the library door and motioned for Franklin to join him. The two men spoke briefly, then the stable master almost ran from the house.

"What is it, Franklin?" Lena asked.

"I sent Edwin to fetch Mr. Corbin, miss. Rupert's horse came back without a rider."

"And Esther's horse?"

"It hasn't returned."

Lena clamped her hand over her mouth to stop the cry that wanted to escape, but she couldn't muffle it. She'd never been so frightened in her life. Essie would be lost without anyone to guide her. She wouldn't know which way to go to get back home. Would her horse wander? Would it find its way back to the stable on its own?

"Franklin, please send some men out to look for Rupert. Something must have happened to him if his horse returned without him."

"Edwin has already sent several men to look for him, miss. I'm sure everything is fine. We should know soon."

"Yes, Franklin," Lena said, trying to convince herself that everything *was* fine.

Suddenly, there was a knock on the front door and Franklin almost ran to see who was there. He wasn't gone long and returned carrying a message.

"This came for you, miss. A lad brought it. I didn't recognize him. He must have been from one of the farms nearby."

Lena took the missive and opened it. The writing was obviously a man's hand—crude and hardly legible. She wondered who could have scribbled so poorly.

Miss Osbourne,

If you ever want to see your sister again, bring ten thousand pounds to the Willowbrook crossroads by noon tomorrow. And come alone. Don't tell Corbin what you are doing or you'll never see your sister again. I'll kill her.

The paper in Lena's hands fluttered to the floor. She stared at it as if it was burning hot and she dared not touch it.

"Are you all right, Miss Magdalena?"

Lena lifted her gaze and stared at Franklin. His mouth moved, but she couldn't quite make out what he said. The only words going around in her head were the last words of the missive. *I'll kill her. I'll kill her.*

I'll kill her.

Lena clamped her hands over her ears to stop the words and the loud commotion coming from beyond the room.

"Lena?" a voice called her.

"No!" she screamed.

"Lena," the voice said again, then again.

Lena tipped her head back to face who was talking to her. It was Jack. Jack was here.

She jumped from the sofa and wrapped her arms around him, clinging to him as if he was the lifeline she needed to save her.

"He has her! He has Essie! He's going to kill her."

"No, he isn't. We won't let him."

"He wants ten thousand pounds, or he said he's going to kill her, Jack."

For the first time, Lena realized that Jack wasn't alone. Brad had come with him. He read the message Barnaby had sent and handed it to Jack.

"He's a dead man, Jack. I'm going to kill him," Brad said.

"It won't come to that," Jack replied. "We'll get Essie back and turn him over to the authorities. They can take care of him."

"No," Brad growled. "I'm going to kill him."

As he spoke, a commotion erupted in the foyer as several

stable hands carried Rupert in on a makeshift stretcher.

"Send someone for Doctor Edwards, Franklin," Jack said.

"That's already taken care of, sir."

"Thank you, Franklin. How is he?"

"Not good, sir. He's been shot, and he's lost a lot of blood."

"Take him to a room and send Cook up to do what she can until the doctor comes."

"Yes, sir."

Lena listened to Jack take control of the situation and was ever so glad he was here. She hugged herself and rocked back and forth on the sofa. She didn't know how she would go through this if he weren't here, and if he weren't the strong leader that he was. She knew at that moment that she loved him. She loved everything about him.

Finally, they were alone. Franklin had gone to do everything Jack had ordered him to, and Brad had gone up to check on Rupert.

Jack went to the sideboard and poured Lena a glass of wine and himself a tumbler of whiskey.

"Here, drink this," he said, holding the glass out to her.

"I'm all right," Lena said, wanting to refuse the wine. She needed to keep her mind clear.

"No, you're not. You're ready to fall apart." He placed the wine in her hand.

Lena took a swallow, then another. She placed the glass on the nearest table, then focused on Jack.

"Jack..." she said. That was the only word she got out before her throat closed and a river of tears streamed from her eyes.

He wrapped his arms around her and held her close. "It's all right to cry, sweetheart."

And she did. She tried to stop the tears from falling and the painful sobs from racking her body, but she couldn't. A fear so uncontrollable consumed her that she knew she had lost the grip on her emotions. And still, Jack held her while he whispered words of comfort. He was the perfect balm to ease her pain.

Finally, Lena was able to stop her tears. "Jack, what am I going to do?"

"*You* aren't going to do anything. *We* are going to take care of this. We're going to do exactly what the message tells us to. We're going to get the money he wants, and you're going to take it to the Willowbrook crossroads at noon and exchange it for your sister."

"But the note said not to tell you what had happened."

"Barnaby won't see me, so he will never know I'm aware that he's taken your sister."

"But I can't allow you to pay the ransom. You can't afford to lose ten thousand pounds. That's more than a month's profit."

"You let me worry about that. You only have to worry about getting Essie back. Can you do that?"

"Yes. Oh, yes."

"That's my brave girl."

"Hold me, Jack. Will you hold me a moment longer?" she asked.

"You know I will. I'll hold you forever and never let you go."

CHAPTER FOURTEEN

J ACK SAT WITH Lena all night and held her close. He hoped she'd fall asleep for at least a little while, but she didn't. From time to time her body trembled and tears streamed down her cheeks. She couldn't cope with what might be happening to Essie.

Jack prayed that Barnaby didn't harm her. He wasn't sure who would blame themselves more if something happened to her—Lena or Brad.

The hours dragged on while Jack and Lena waited for the sun to rise so they could go to the bank to withdraw the ten thousand pounds that Barnaby had demanded. But time seemed to crawl ever so slowly.

"Would you like a cup of tea?" Jack asked her when a parlor maid brought in a fresh tray.

Lena only nodded.

He poured a cup and held it out for her to take, but her hands shook so violently that she couldn't hold the cup steady. Jack held it for her and helped her when she wanted to take a sip.

"I'm sorry I'm not stronger, Jack. But I can't help but feel that I failed Essie. Before she died, my mother made me promise that I would take care of my sister. That I wouldn't let anything happen to her. And I failed her," she said as her voice broke and tears ran down her cheeks. "I failed her."

"Shh, sweetheart. You didn't fail her. If anyone failed her, it was me."

"You?" she asked. "How can you think you were at fault?"

"Because I should have seen this coming. I should have realized that if Barnaby was desperate for money, he would do something drastic to get it. I just didn't think he would involve Essie."

"You couldn't have known, Jack. None of us could have."

"No, but I was looking in the wrong direction. I posted extra guards at the club, thinking that he might try to rob us, but I should have known he wasn't brave enough to expose himself to something so dangerous."

"Do you know where Brad is?" she asked.

"Not for sure, but I think he went back to the club. He's taking this as hard as you are, Lena. I think he has grown quite attached to your sister."

"Yes, and my sister has grown quite fond of him." She took another sip of her tea, then focused her gaze out the window. "The sky is getting lighter. The sun will be up soon."

"Yes, sweetheart. It won't be long before we get Essie back with us."

"Oh, Jack. I can't imagine how frightened she is."

"Why don't you get ready to leave? We'll go to the club and collect Brad, then go to the bank to get the money we'll need. But first I want to send someone to London to inform Wilson Hanover what his nephew has done. I think he needs to know."

"The news will upset him," Lena said.

"I'm sure it will, but he's aware of what his nephew has become and encouraged him to change, to no avail."

Jack sat with Lena in his arms a few more minutes, then she got to her feet and went to her room to get ready to leave. After she had changed her clothes, she returned to where Jack was waiting for her, and they went to the club to collect Brad. It was obvious that he hadn't slept the night before either.

"Are you ready to go?" Brad asked.

"Yes," Jack answered, then asked for someone to bring up a

flask of coffee. It was obvious that Brad hadn't only been awake all night, but that he'd spent a great deal of that time drinking.

When the coffee came, Jack poured two cups and handed one of them to Brad, who took a swallow and shivered. "How old is this?" he said in disgust. "It's horrible."

"It's not that bad," Jack said, taking a swallow from his cup. "You've been drinking whiskey so long your palate can't tell a good cup of coffee from a bad one."

Brad groaned again but took another swallow. "How are we going to handle this?" he said when he finished his coffee.

"Lena is going to go in the carriage, and George will drive her. We'll ride along with her and have George let us off a good mile from the crossroads."

"I think we should get out earlier," Brad said. "The countryside there is so flat, Barnaby will be able to see more than a mile."

Jack nodded his agreement. "We'll leave plenty early so George doesn't have to get too close, and Lena will have time to walk a half-mile or so. Can you do that, Lena?"

"Yes. Barnaby has to think I came alone," she replied.

"That's right," Jack said, reaching for her hand and holding it. "We'll put the money in the satchel Brad and I use to go to the bank. It has a thick strap on it that will be long enough to put over your head on your right side and rest on your left hip. Clench your hand around the strap and don't let it go. That should keep it secure."

Lena nodded her understanding.

"Wait for Barnaby to arrive. He should come in a carriage. That will be the easiest to transport Essie. Make sure he has her with him. Don't hand over the money until she is out of the carriage and standing beside you. Only then are you to give him the money. Do you understand?"

"Yes," Lena answered.

"All right," Jack said. "Let's go, then."

They rose from their chairs, and Jack opened a locked closet and removed several weapons from a safe in the wall.

"You kept your gun from the war," Brad said, watching Jack put it into his jacket pocket.

"I thought it might come in handy someday, and this is the day. I have yours, too."

He reached back into the hidden safe and took out another weapon, handing this one to Brad.

"Why did you wait until now to give it to me?"

"Same reason I kept mine hidden."

Brad took the gun and rubbed his hand over it. "I thought maybe you were afraid I might use it to blow my brains out," he said mischievously.

"Well, there was that," Jack said, and Lena clamped her hand over her mouth and gave a muffled groan.

"Now, see what you did?" Jack teased.

"I didn't do anything," Brad said, tucking his gun in his jacket pocket. "You're the one who—"

"Are you finally ready?" Jack interrupted, to change the subject.

Brad left the room first, and Jack and Lena followed.

⤚⟫⟪⟞

IT TOOK A lot longer at the bank than Lena thought it would. She was glad they'd left early.

"Did you have trouble?" she asked when they finally returned.

"Not trouble, exactly," Jack replied. "But because of the large amount, the teller called in the bank president to make sure everything was correct. Then they had to recheck the amount as verification."

"We bring in massive deposits every day," Brad said, obviously frustrated. "You'd think they'd take us at our word."

"They are just being careful," Lena said, wanting to calm the situation.

Finally, they were on their way. Jack let the carriage travel part of the way to the Willowbrook crossroads, then ordered George to stop. They all got out, and Jack helped Lena put the satchel strap on her shoulder.

"This is going to be heavy," he said. "Support it with your opposite hand."

Lena did as she was told.

"Now, take your time, but walk to the Willowbrook crossroads and wait until Barnaby comes. Brad and I will be right behind you. Just remember, don't hand over the money until you have Essie with you."

"I understand," she said, and turned to leave him.

For some reason he didn't understand, he didn't want to let her go. A small voice told him if he let her leave him now, he might never get her back.

"Lena," he said, and pulled her into his arms. "I love you." He lowered his head and kissed her. His kiss was deep and filled with all the passion he felt, exemplifying the depth of his love for her.

He lifted his head and broke their kiss.

"And I love you, Jack. More than you will ever know."

Lena stepped out of his arms and started her walk to get her sister back.

Jack wanted to go after her but couldn't. There was nothing he could do but watch her walk away from him.

LENA CLUTCHED AT the satchel with the money that would get Essie back. She would follow the note's instructions to the letter. She couldn't lose her sister. She couldn't break the promise she'd made to her mother. If she lost Essie, it would be like losing a part of herself.

She trudged along the road until she could see the sign that indicated she'd reached the Willowbrook crossing, and stopped.

She wasn't sure how long she would have to wait, but she'd wait forever if it meant she would have Essie back with her.

Time seemed to stop while she waited. Lena had no idea how long she'd stood there, staring down the long road where the carriage carrying Essie would come. But it seemed like forever.

Finally, she saw it. A carriage came down the road at a slow crawl.

Her heart pounded in her breast, and she prayed that everything would go as expected and this ordeal would be over. She clutched the shoulder satchel so fiercely it left imprints in her palm. She tried to move but couldn't. Her gaze remained frozen on the carriage inching closer to her.

Then the carriage stopped, and the door opened.

This was it. She was about to see Essie again. She was about to see the man who had taken her sister for the money to repay his gambling debts. How could Josiah Barnaby possibly think Essie's life was worth the mere ten thousand pounds he had gambled and lost?

Lena disliked Barnaby more at that moment than she thought she could dislike anyone. If he were close enough to her, she feared she might scratch his eyes out and make him as blind as Essie.

But that wouldn't get her sister back. That wouldn't be what God would want her to do. Instead, she watched as the carriage door opened and a man descended.

Lena looked at him in confusion. Something was wrong. This wasn't how she thought it would be.

"Do you have my money?" he demanded.

"Do you have my sister?" Lena asked.

The man laughed.

"CAN YOU SEE them?" a man asked sotto voce behind them.

Jack and Brad spun around to face the speaker and froze with their guns aimed at the man's chest.

"What the hell?" Jack and Brad said in unison.

The man held his hands up in surrender. "Not who you expected, am I?"

"No!" Jack answered, staring at Josiah Barnaby. "Then who is in the carriage? Who kidnapped Essie?"

Barnaby looked in the direction Brad and Jack indicated. "No doubt my uncle," he said in a sober voice. "One of my men has been suspicious about what he's been up to," he said to Jack. "You might have saved her life."

"But your uncle said—"

"I know. He told you I was the one with the huge gambling problem and he was trying to help me become a better man."

"Yes," Jack replied, turning back to where Lena stood on the road.

"Has she given Hanover the money yet?"

"No. She still has it."

"Good. Are either of you adequate shots?"

"I'm fair," Jack answered, "but Brad is excellent."

"I'll take you, then," Barnaby said to Brad. "Stay in the weeds on the side of the road and try not to let my uncle see you." He turned to Jack. "Keep your eyes on Hanover."

"What are you going to do?" Brad asked.

"Just follow me and you'll see."

Jack and Brad shared a concerned glance, then Brad followed Barnaby as he walked toward his uncle.

"What are you up to, Uncle?" he yelled.

"What are you doing here?" a startled Hanover bellowed.

"I came to help you," Barnaby said, raising his hands. "See, I'm unarmed. I'm not a threat to you."

"Get out of here! I don't need your help. I never have. It's my meddling sister who thinks I do. If it weren't for your mother, I'd be living the life I wanted."

"No, if it weren't for my mother, you'd be rotting in debtor's prison."

"You don't know what you're talking about. My luck is about to change anytime now."

"Your luck is never going to change, Uncle. You've always been a pathetic card player, and you are getting worse."

"How dare you!"

"I dare because my mother loves you, although I don't know why, and I want to help you."

"No, you don't. You only want my money."

"What money? You're broke, Uncle. You're destitute! That's why you've resorted to kidnapping a helpless female who is blind and blackmailing her sister to pay you enough money to cover your debts."

"I had to," Hanover said. "You don't know the men I owe money to! They're dangerous men! They'll kill me if I don't pay what I owe them."

"Then let me help you."

"How?"

"We'll go back to London, and I'll help you get a loan from the bank to cover your vowels. In return, you'll promise me that the only person you will ever gamble against is me. I might even let you win once in a while."

"Ha!" his uncle said, a bit of hysteria in his laugh.

Jack listened to the exchange and was impressed by Barnaby's understanding.

"You are such a fool if you think I'm going to agree to that kind of life, Josiah," Hanover said, then lifted his gun and shot his nephew in the arm. "Now, Miss Osbourne, give me the money!"

"Give me my sister first!" Lena yelled.

HANOVER TURNED AND pulled Essie out of the carriage.

Lena looked at her sister and fought the lump that settled in her throat. Essie's hair was disheveled, and her gown was wrinkled and stained with dirt. It was obvious that she'd slept on the floor of a barn, or the floor of the carriage, and Lena doubted she'd been fed.

She wanted to run to Essie and take her in her arms, but she remembered what Jack had told her.

Don't hand over the money until she is out of the carriage and standing beside you. Only then are you to give him the money.

"Give me the money!" Hanover bellowed again.

"Send over my sister first! Essie, come to me! Walk straight ahead. About twenty-four steps."

Essie took her first step toward Lena, then a second, but without warning, Hanover lifted his pistol and aimed it at Essie.

"No!" Lena screamed, and ran to shield her sister. She stepped in front of Essie and held on to her with all her might.

"No!" Brad bellowed, then he fired his gun. His bullet went through Hanover's heart.

"No!" Jack bellowed at the same time, then he fired his gun. His bullet struck Hanover in the gut.

⇻⤞⤝⇺

JACK DIDN'T TAKE time to see if Hanover was dead. He knew he was, the same as he knew Lena had been shot.

"Sweetheart!" he called out, dropping to the ground where Lena had fallen.

"Jack," she whispered, struggling to keep her eyes open.

"Don't talk, sweetheart."

"Brad!" Essie screamed. "Where's Lena? What happened?"

"Hush, darling," Brad whispered, holding Essie to his chest and kissing her. "Lena's been hurt, but she'll be fine. Hang on to me. We're going to get her to a doctor."

"We need to hurry, Brad."

"Yes, darling. We will."

Just then, George arrived with the carriage. He jumped down

and opened the door so Jack could step in with Lena. Brad helped Essie inside. "Barnaby!" he yelled. "Get in. You need to see a doctor, too."

"I can't leave my uncle here alone," Barnaby said. "Send someone back to help me."

"I will," Brad replied. George slapped the reins, and the horses surged forward.

Jack pressed his hand against Lena's wound to help stop the bleeding as he repeatedly told her that she was going to be all right, that Essie was safe. That Lena had kept her promise to her mother.

Except Jack was afraid Lena didn't hear him.

CHAPTER FIFTEEN

"I F YOU CONTINUE as you have been, you're going to have to hire me full time," Doctor Edwards told Jack after he'd taken care of everyone who had been shot the last two days.

"Hopefully, we won't have more days like this. I haven't seen the like since the war."

"At least you didn't see as many fatalities this time as you saw during the war."

"No," Jack replied. "I've seen enough death in my life that I don't need to see any more. Can I offer you something to drink and a little something to fill your stomach?"

"I would appreciate that," Doctor Edwards said. "I think Miss Osbourne will sleep for a while yet, and her sister is here if she needs anything."

"You are sure Lena will be all right?" Jack asked, looking to the bed where Lena slept. Essie sat in a chair beside the bed and held her sister's hand.

"I'm positive. The bullet went through her shoulder and came out clean. It didn't hit anything vital. She was very lucky."

"Then I'll go down with you, but I can't stay long."

"No, but I would like to speak with you. I have some questions about what exactly happened in case the magistrate asks me."

"Of course. Come with me," Jack said, and headed for the

door. He and Doctor Edwards descended to Jack's study. "Brandy or whiskey?" Jack asked.

"Brandy."

Jack poured two glasses of brandy and handed the doctor one. Before they'd taken their first swallows, the door opened and Brad entered.

"Join us, Brad," Jack said, and Brad poured himself a tumbler of whiskey.

"Like I said," Doctor Edwards continued, "I think it's wise that I know what happened so if I'm asked, everything will make sense."

"Yes," Jack agreed. "I have to start back when it was first decided the railroad would come through Willowbrook. Wilson Hanover had controlling interest in the London line of the railroad. At least, his family did."

"Am I correct that he is the man who died from gunshot wounds?"

"Yes. Brad and I shot him."

"Very well. Please, go on."

"When Hanover first arrived, he gave us the impression that he ran the company and had taken his nephew, Josiah Barnaby, under his wing to curb his gambling problem."

"But that wasn't the truth?" Doctor Edwards asked.

"No. In reality, Hanover was the one with the gambling problem. He owed thousands of pounds to several gaming halls and money lenders, and they were demanding payment of his debts."

"Am I correct in assuming that he didn't have the money to meet their demands?"

"Yes. He was able to make payments by overcharging for the supplies and materials on previous railroad projects. But when the Willowbrook investors decided we should buy as much of what we needed here in town and pay the bills ourselves, Hanover could no longer steal from the company."

"And he was desperate for a new source of funds," Doctor

Edwards said.

"Yes. One of our stable hands was teaching Essie to ride, and Hanover shot the stable hand and kidnapped her."

"That stable hand was the first bullet wound I treated, wasn't it?"

"Yes. And to get the money he needed, Hanover sent a ransom note for ten thousand pounds. Lena was to meet Hanover at the Willowbrook crossroads this morning to give him the money and get Essie in return."

"I take it, though, that things didn't go as planned."

"Hanover led us to believe that Barnaby was the one with a gambling problem, and he was the one who had kidnapped Essie. Lena was instructed not to tell anyone about the kidnapping or the money, but she came to me for help."

"That was smart. How did Hanover think Lena would get that much money?"

"He expected her to steal it."

"That was a futile demand. Her father was the vicar here for years. She wouldn't steal it. That went against everything she'd been taught."

"Yes," Jack said, knowing instinctively that was true. Lena would never steal because she'd been taught it was wrong to take anything that wasn't hers.

"I have one more question. Who shot Barnaby?"

"Hanover. Barnaby offered to take out a loan for his uncle for the amount he owed on the condition that he stop gambling, but Hanover refused. When Barnaby told his uncle that was the only way he would get the money, he became angry and shot his nephew."

Doctor Edwards shook his head. "What an experience you have had."

"Yes," Jack said, then got to his feet. "But now I need to get back to Lena. She should be waking anytime now." He called for Franklin. "Take Doctor Edwards to the kitchen, Franklin, and have Cook feed him. We've worked him hard enough. He deserves some of her home-cooked food."

"Yes, sir," Franklin said, then took the doctor to the kitchen.

"Are you coming up with me, Brad?" Jack asked his friend.

"Yes. I need to stay close to Essie. She hasn't had time to process much of what happened in the last two days. She's been so brave through it all, and I'm afraid she needs a shoulder to lean on."

"Yes, I'm sure she does," Jack said, then walked up the stairs with Brad beside him.

When they entered the bedroom, Essie still sat beside Lena, holding her hand.

"How is she?" Jack asked.

"She's more restless than earlier," Essie replied.

"That means she's probably waking. Brad's here," he said. "Go with him. You need something to eat—and someone to talk to."

"Perhaps you are correct," Essie said, releasing Lena's hand and rising. Brad wrapped his arm around Essie and led her from the room.

Jack sat where Essie had been and reached for Lena's hand. She thrashed her head back and forth on the pillow and released a painful moan.

"Don't move, Lena," he said, placing a hand on her shoulder to keep her from doing damage to the stitches Doctor Edwards had put in.

"Jack?" she whispered.

"Yes, sweetheart. I'm right here."

"Are you all right?"

He smiled. "I'm fine. You are the one who was hurt. You and Josiah Barnaby."

"Is Hanover dead?"

"Yes, Lena. He's dead."

"I know I shouldn't be, but I'm glad."

"You can be glad, sweetheart. He did enough damage and would have continued doing more had he lived."

"I know."

"Would you like something for the pain?"

"Will it make me sleep?"

"Yes, probably."

"Then no. I'll wait a little while."

Jack rose from his chair and sat beside her on the bed. "Very well, but don't talk. I'll talk to you."

"Is Essie all right?"

"Yes, she's fine. She just left with Brad. They went to get something to eat."

"Good."

"Did you think for a minute that the culprit was Hanover and not Barnaby?"

"No."

"Neither did I. Hanover had me totally fooled. He convinced me that his nephew was the one with the gambling problem, and I didn't even question it."

"No one did. How is he?"

"He's resting. He wasn't hurt badly. The doctor said he was very lucky. He'll be up in a day or two."

"Good."

Jack got up and mixed a small amount of laudanum with a little wine. "Here," he said, holding it to her mouth. "Drink this. I can tell you are in more pain, and you're ready to fall asleep."

Lena drank, then closed her eyes and fell asleep.

Jack leaned over and kissed her cheek, then held her hand while he sat in the chair and watched her sleep.

LENA SLOWLY OPENED her eyes and tried to focus on her surroundings. The sun was up, so she knew it was past daybreak, but not by much. She turned her head and focused on Jack sleeping in the chair beside her bed. His hair was unkempt, not combed as neatly as she was used to seeing. Lena smiled. She rather liked it like this.

He still held her hand, the same as he had when she fell asleep last night. She couldn't believe how much she loved him. Couldn't believe how grateful she was that he loved her. He was the best thing that had ever happened in her life.

She didn't want to startle him awake, so she made slow, lazy circles with her thumb on the top of his hand until he stirred. His eyes opened ever so slowly until his startling blue gaze landed on her.

"Good morning, Jack," she whispered.

"Good morning, Lena. You are looking much better than you did last night."

"I feel much better than I did last night," she replied. "You didn't have to sit in that chair all night. You could have found a bed and slept more comfortably."

"And leave you alone? Not likely."

"How is everyone?"

"Essie and Brad are together."

"Together?"

"I'm afraid so, darling. I regret that I wasn't a very watchful chaperone. I may have to insist on the banns being read."

Lena tried to laugh but stopped when a stabbing pain traveled down her arm. "I don't believe it."

"Oh, believe it. I don't think they spent all their time every afternoon reading. They might have been occupied with one or two activities more enjoyable than working their way through my library."

"How did I not know?" Lena asked. "I didn't even think…"

"That's because you were so busy counting money and entering numbers in the ledgers."

"Oh, Jack. What are we going to do? I need to heal quickly. The club will be—"

"The club will be just fine. Brad will take over making out a deposit each day, and we'll leave the ledgers for you to work on when you are completely healed."

"How is Barnaby?"

"Much better. He will need to rest for a few days, then he'll be traveling back to London. He said he needs to be with his mother. This has been quite a shock to her."

"I can imagine. And what about Rupert?"

"Doctor Edwards said he's out of danger but still needs to be watched, and get plenty of rest."

"I can't believe Hanover intended to kill all of us," Lena said.

"I can't believe that he thought he could get away with it," Jack said.

"I don't think he was thinking clearly. I believe he was so desperate to get his hands on the money he needed to pay his creditors that he didn't see the flaws in his plan."

"I think you are right."

Just then, the door opened and Lena's maid came in with a tray of tea and toasted bread.

"You are just in time," Jack said. "I think your mistress needs your help. I'll carry her to the closet, and you can take over from there. Just call when you need me to take her back to bed."

"Yes, sir," the maid said, then Jack carried Lena to the closet and left her to do her morning ablutions. When she was finished, she had a cup of tea and considered everything Jack told her.

Her baby sister wasn't a baby any longer. She was going to get married.

CHAPTER SIXTEEN

L ENA SAT AT the desk in Jack's study and entered numbers in the ledgers Jack had brought from the club.

It had been four weeks since Essie had been kidnapped and Lena had been shot. She was much improved and almost ready to return to the club to work, but Jack wouldn't let her yet. He told her it was too soon.

Most days she felt fine and was sure she could work all day. Then there were days when she was ready to rest by noon. But today she was sure she could work well into the night, she felt so energized.

Jack would never allow that, though. He kept a close watch on her and made sure she didn't overdo it.

Brad and Essie were married a week ago. They had a small yet beautiful celebration. Essie, of course, made a beautiful bride, and Brad was an extremely handsome groom. Lena was so happy for them. To her chagrin, she cried through the entire ceremony. She couldn't believe Essie had found the perfect man to marry, a man who loved her with his whole heart despite her blindness. That was something she'd never thought would happen.

Jack had insisted that Brad and Essie live at Corbin House. Brad had always lived in the west wing, and Jack offered to enlarge it to make it as big as Essie and Brad wanted, but Essie had refused his offer. She explained that she felt more comfortable in a smaller space. That would be easier for her to manage. Brad agreed, so they moved their meager belongings into the west wing and made their home there.

Jack still slept at the club, and Lena slept in her room in the east wing. She loved it here, and if Jack ever proposed, this was where they would live.

"Are you gathering wool again, Lena?" Jack said from the doorway of his study.

Lena laughed. "Yes," she answered. "I think we should invest in some sheep. I find I gather wool so often, sheep would be quite profitable."

Jack laughed, then crossed the room and came around the desk to kiss her. "Oh, you smell good. What did you have for breakfast?"

"Toasted bread with orange marmalade. It was delicious."

"Now, you are delicious."

"And you are a flatterer."

"Of course I am. It's what I'm known for."

"I can believe that. What am I ever going to do with you?"

"You are going to get up from that chair and come over to the sofa and talk to me. I have something to tell you about."

Lena rose from her chair and walked to the sofa, where she sat down beside him. "What? Has something happened?"

"I had a visitor this morning."

"Who?"

"Josiah Barnaby came to see me."

"Oh, how is he doing?"

"Physically, he's doing fine. But he is thinking about bringing his mother and moving to Willowbrook."

"That's wonderful, isn't it?"

"Yes, but he needs something to do, and all he's ever done is build railroads with his uncle."

"So, what are his intentions?"

"He wanted to know if I would be interested in his taking over the running of the London/Willowbrook line."

"Oh," Lena answered, trying to be noncommittal. "What do you think of that? Would you be interested in giving up controlling interest? It would mean a loss of income for you."

"It would mean a loss of income for *us*," he corrected her.

"Money has never been that important to me, Jack. You know that. I have an idea of the money you make, and it's far more than we will ever need."

"So, you are in favor of letting Barnaby manage the railroad line?"

Lena turned on the sofa to squarely face him. "I would be in favor of you deciding what you would like to do, Jack. You would have more time to enjoy running your club, and more time to enjoy being with your wife and children—should you ever have them."

"Are you saying that I may not?" he asked with a look of surprise on his face.

"I don't know," Lena teased. "I wasn't aware that you had asked anyone to be your bride."

"I guess I haven't. I will have to remedy that. Will you marry me, Lena?"

Her eyes filled with tears of happiness. "Well, since you are the only man I have ever loved, or ever will love, I suppose I probably should marry you."

"Yes, I suppose you should," he said, "and since I purchased a special license the last time I went to London, we should probably get married before it expires."

"Yes, we probably should," Lena said. "Because I imagine it cost you a great deal of money."

"Oh, it did," Jack teased. "But then, you are worth it."

"Oh, I am," Lena assured him as another tear streamed down her cheek.

"I love you, Lena," Jack said, holding her in his arms. "More than I thought I would ever love anyone."

"We will have a wonderful life together, Jack. A life filled with happiness and laughter and lots of children to love."

"How many is 'lots'?" he asked.

"I don't know. However many God grants us. He knows we have lots of love to give them."

"Yes, we do," he said, and kissed her.

EPILOGUE

THE SUN HADN'T peeked over the horizon, but the sky wasn't as dark as it had been a few minutes before, so Lena knew it wouldn't be long before Jack was awake. She blamed his early waking time each morning to his years in the army, but she didn't mind. It was their habit to start their day making love. She loved that about married life.

She and Jack had been married almost five months now, with every day revealing itself to be more special than the day before. And the coming days were going to be even more so.

Lena smiled, and Jack shifted beneath her. After they made love last night, she had fallen asleep with her cheek on Jack's chest. At first, she listened to his heart rush from the exertion of making love to her. Then his heart gradually slowed, and finally he fell asleep. After that, the steady beating of his heart lulled *her* to sleep.

She smiled again thinking of how happy she was, how blessed.

"Are you gathering wool again, sweetheart?"

"Did I wake you?"

"Yes, but I don't mind. It's almost time to get up."

"No, it isn't," she replied.

"Oh, do you have something else in mind?"

"Yes, I'd like to talk to you."

"Well, that's not exactly what *I* had in mind," he complained.

"I know what you had in mind, and maybe we can get around to that later."

"Promise?"

"Maybe," she teased.

"Very well. What would you like to talk about?"

"I had an idea I want to discuss with you. I've had it for quite a while already but forgot about it until just lately."

Jack turned to his side. He rested his head on his palm and looked down on her. There was a frown on his face, which meant he was taking her seriously. "What idea is that?"

"What do you think about opening a second club?"

"A second club! Are you serious?"

"Yes. But this club will be called Jackson's Ladies' Club."

"A *ladies'* club?"

"Yes. A ladies' club."

"And what would these ladies do at their club?"

"Why, the exact same thing that gentlemen do at their club: sit together in little clusters and discuss the events of the day. Play whist. Or even chess. The club will provide refreshments, either tea or lemonade, or even a glass of wine. And there will be cakes or something more filling. Some of the women might come to read the newspaper or do their correspondence without being interrupted. And, of course, some ladies might come to go to the gaming room and play cards. Several of them might even enjoy gambling."

"Gambling?"

"Yes, Jack. It might shock you to know that some ladies enjoy games of chance equally as much as men. In my experience, it takes a good deal of skill to make a decent wager."

"And not much at all to make a bad one."

"But we'd school the ladies, darling. We'd teach them the strategies and encourage caution. It might help some be more understanding of their husband's interest, don't you think?"

Jack shifted onto his back and thrust his hands behind his

head.

He was considering her idea. That was a good sign.

"Who would run this club?"

"Well, we would have to hire someone. I would help out when I could, but I won't be available to run the club full time."

"And why won't you?"

"Well, that happens to be the second thing I wanted to discuss with you."

"Another idea? You have *another* idea?"

"Actually, no. The idea was yours."

"Mine?"

"Yes. What did you think would happen when you woke up early every morning feeling, well, shall we say, *frisky?*"

"Well, I thought—" Jack stopped talking and sat up. "I thought… Are you… Are you sure?"

Lena laughed. "Yes, I'm sure."

"Oh my," he said, leaning close to her and kissing her. "How long have you known?"

"About eight weeks. We should welcome your son or daughter sometime before Christmas."

"Christmas," Jack said with a sigh. "I'm going to be a father for Christmas. I can't believe it."

"I take it you are happy about the news?" Lena said, looking at the glow on his face.

"Oh, Lena. I couldn't be happier. I never thought I'd be a father. There were times during the war when I doubted I'd survive long enough to make it back to Britain, let alone anything past that. Then I met Lord Murdock, and he offered me the money to start Jackson's. Then I met you and fell in love. That's when I let myself dream of a home and a family." Jack gathered her into his arms and held her close. "You asked if I was happy. That's hardly the word for it. I'm ecstatic, darling. Completely ecstatic."

"So, in your elation, might you also think about starting a ladies' club, even if I won't be able to devote all my time to running it?"

"Of course I will. I will think about anything you suggest. You haven't led me wrong since I met you. I doubt you will start now."

"Oh, I love you, Jack. More than I can ever say."

"I shall never tire of hearing it, my love." He kissed her soundly. "Never."

About the Author

Laura Landon taught high school for ten years before leaving the classroom to open her own ice-cream shop. As much as she loved serving up sundaes and malts from behind the counter, she closed up shop after penning her first novel. Now she spends nearly every waking minute writing, guiding her heroes and heroines to find their happily ever afters.

She is the author of more than a dozen historical novels, including SILENT REVENGE, INTIMATE DECEPTION, and her newest Montlake Romance release, INTIMATE SURREN-DER.

Her books are enjoyed by readers around the world.